THE LANGUAGE OF HOME

stories

ALSO BY THE AUTHOR

FICTION

Widower, 48, Seeks Husband | Compassion, Michigan

Flannelwood | The Last Deaf Club in America

The Kinda Fella I Am | Men with Their Hands

POETRY

Ironhood | Animals Out-There W-i-l-d

Far from Atlantis | Lunafly | once upon a twin

Chlorophyll | Bokeh Focus | A Babble of Objects

The Kiss of Walt Whitman Still on My Lips | How to Kill Poetry

Road Work Ahead | Mute | This Way to the Acorns | St. Michael's Fall

PROSE

A Quiet Foghorn: More Notes from a Deaf Gay Life

From Heart into Art: Interviews with
Deaf and Hard of Hearing Artists and Their Allies

Notes of a Deaf Gay Writer: 20 Years Later

Whispers of a Savage Sort and Other Plays about the Deaf American Experience

Assembly Required: Notes from a Deaf Gay Life

Snooty: A Comedy

Silence Is a Four-Letter Word: On Art & Deafness

AS EDITOR

I'll Tell You Later: Deaf Survivors of Dinner Table Syndrome

Oh Yeah: A Bear Poetry Anthology

Yooper Poetry: On Experiencing Michigan's Upper Peninsula

Lovejets: Queer Male Poets on 200 Years of Walt Whitman

QDA: A Queer Disability Anthology

Among the Leaves: Queer Male Poets on the Midwestern Experience

Eyes of Desire 2: A Deaf GLBT Reader

When I Am Dead: The Writings of George M. Teegarden

Eyes of Desire: A Deaf Gay & Lesbian Reader

ADVANCE PRAISE FOR

The Language of Home: Stories

"*The Language of Home* is a moving collection of stories written by one of our most important contemporary Deaf writers. Luczak's work is a tender, humorous, and lyrical offering of sharp truths about the lives of the Deaf."

—Raymond Antrobus,
author of *The Quiet Ear: An Investigation of Missing Sound: A Memoir*

"Raymond Luczak writes for us—the Us who are, to most nondisabled people, Them, the Other. In *The Language of Home,* he writes for Deaf readers first, and the rest of us, recognizing some of the struggle, are swept along. He writes in a series of short stories and vignettes like flashes of lightning that throw shadows at slant and sharp angles, rendering the ordinary newly strange, immersing us in the lived experience of his deaf (and Deaf) characters as they move through a sometimes hostile world.

These people—the little deaf girl who survives a terrible confusion to save her sister, lose her family, but find her real home, language; the girl then wife then mother embedded so deep in her Deaf community that all friends and enemies, gossips and lovers are Deaf—become, to the reader, simply people. Not inspiring or admirable, not brilliant or strange, just ... people. People living their lives as we all do. Sometimes resisting and surviving a world that doesn't want us, and sometimes squabbling among the loving friends and family of a tightly-knit community.

But always, and above all, Luczak writes for Us—all of us. *The Language of Home* is not for a small, specialized readership, it belongs in every library and on every bookshelf. Its warmth and generosity will enfold and draw in any reader eager to enter into the lives of those we don't know—to walk alongside them, feeling what they feel, understanding what they understand, becoming them, just for a little while."

—Nicola Griffith,
multiple award-winning author of *Hild, Spear,* and *So Lucky*

THE LANGUAGE OF HOME

stories

RAYMOND LUCZAK

Gallaudet University Press
Washington, DC

Library of Congress Cataloging-in-Publication Data

Names: Luczak, Raymond, 1965- author.
Title: The language of home : stories / Raymond Luczak.
Description: Washington, DC : Gallaudet University Press, 2025. | Summary: "This short story collection offers an authentic, unflinching exploration of Deaf identity and community via a variety of d/Deaf characters based in the United States"-- Provided by publisher.
Identifiers: LCCN 2024059804 (print) | LCCN 2024059805 (ebook) | ISBN 9781954622678 (paperback) | ISBN 9781954622685 (ebook)
Subjects: LCSH: Deaf people--Fiction. | LCGFT: Short stories.
Classification: LCC PS3562.U2554 L36 2025 (print) | LCC PS3562.U2554 (ebook) | DDC 813/.54--dc23/eng/20250106
LC record available at https://lccn.loc.gov/2024059804
LC ebook record available at https://lccn.loc.gov/2024059805

Gallaudet University Press
Washington, DC 20002
gupress.gallaudet.edu

Gallaudet University Press is located on the traditional territories of Nacotchtank and Piscataway.

Printed in the United States of America

ISBN: 978-1-954622-67-8 (paperback)
ISBN: 978-1-954622-68-5 (ebook)

∞ This paper meets the requirements of ANSI/NISO Z39.48–1992 (Permanence of Paper).

Cover description: Against an off-white wall lit brightly from above, a heavily varnished brown wooden chair is set before a table that's equally heavily varnished. Before the chair is a white plate with two slender circles painted right near the plate's edge. On either side of the plate is a silver fork and knife; on the left side of the plate is an empty glass. Higher up on the wall above the chair is the following text in dark red: THE LANGUAGE OF HOME; stories; Raymond Luczak.

Cover design by Mona Z. Kraculdy.

in memory of
Melainie Wilding Garcia (1964–2022),
who was there from the very day
I began spinning these tales

CONTENTS

A NOTE TO THE READER

Please be aware that the acronym for American Sign Language is "ASL" and that when the word "Deaf" is capitalized, it refers to deaf people as a social and linguistic group that use sign language to communicate as opposed to deaf people who don't sign. Some signed dialogue uses ASL gloss.

In addition, references to audism, ableism, homophobia, and sexual assault are present in this collection, as well as strong language. Readers who may be sensitive to these elements, please take note.

stories

THE LANGUAGE OF HOME

You are a young girl named Melinda—six or seven years old, perhaps—hearing only certain sounds with the help of your shiny, metallic hearing aid nestled inside a snug-fitting harness over your chest. The two tiny cords curling their way up to your earmolds have the same color as your skin. When you do not hear anything, you sometimes bang on the box at your chest so that you will hear something. And today you can hear, without needing to turn up the volume, your sister Una screaming from your bedroom.

The first time you hear this you are not sure what it is. It does not sound anything like the "Ba ba ba!" your speech therapist encourages you to make every day at school; you know you are one of her best students because you always demand to know the location of each sound that you hear. Your speech therapist has excused the fact that you are way behind in your speech progress because your father is a migrant apple picker working all over the Northwest, taking his family along, and so you never had a chance to follow a consistent line of action. There were too many therapists, too many schools, too many approaches geared to make you talk. But you possess a clear "Ba!"

So you scamper upstairs in search of that sound. It's a game; you hope Una will give you some Froot Loops when you identify the sound correctly. You cannot wait to see Una smile and hug you with kisses on your slightly freckled cheeks. And she will ask you if you want your brown hair rebraided. You will nod *YesYesYes,* not caring how you look as long as Una plays with your hair in front of the mirror. At fifteen, Una is the oldest.

The first door in the hallway you see is the bathroom. It is open and empty. You see the toilet and you remember how clumsy it still is to get up on the seat to potty. But you know practice makes perfect, and Una doesn't have to worry so much about you falling in backwards when Mama lies quietly on the couch in front of the

TV. Mama coughs occasionally but at least she covers her mouth whenever you come in. You have often watched Mama rearrange her tiny brown plastic pillboxes into some mysterious order on the coffee table, perhaps in search of some magical sequence that will make her young and healthy again.

You leave the bathroom and notice your brother Ern's door is closed. You force your hearing aid toward it, the way you had seen Ern cupping his ear against a door somewhere a long time ago. You have forgotten in which house that happened; your family has moved too many times. You hear that sound again, but you cannot tell where it's coming from. You reach up, turn the knob, and push the door open, expecting to find a rustle of movement in response to your invasion.

Instead, Ern is covering his ears with two of his pillows atop his bed. His eyes are closed very tightly; you wonder if he is having a bad dream. You put your eyebrows together, trying to decide whether Ern is enjoying himself or not. He is four years older than you. He never says much. But he always makes sure your hearing aid is turned off at night. If he forgets, no one else does. The feedback from your hearing aid always reminds someone in your house to conserve its battery for another day. And if you wear it at night, your body is sore because you always turn over all night, like French toast. You look again at Ern, wondering what could bother him so much. But he hates explaining anything to you. He does not like noise or the Buddy Holly records Mama puts on the phonograph player whenever Dada is out picking.

You turn around and close his door quietly. The door across from Ern's is a closet door where towels and toilet paper are kept. You feel afraid because you remember hiding there all night when you first moved here. Mama had been very nervous all that day—you could tell from her ragged fingernails and her bony hands shaking as she sat quietly smoking while you and Dada and Una and Ern carried boxes into the house. Mama and Dada began screaming at each other, and you saw Dada throw a lamp at Mama as Una grabbed and carried you upstairs. You remember how carefully Una touched your hair and how frightened her eyes appeared. You didn't have your new hearing aid then, but you clustered your eyebrows together to ask Una why Mama and Dada were fighting. As Una hugged you, she opened the closet door and hid you there.

For a long while you felt the floor's vibrations. Your body felt the angry storm of Dada's feet. You longed for the caressing stride of Una's feet coming to check up on you now and then. Ern's feet are not as obvious: He is almost a ghost. He hides with library books whenever he can. You have been obsessed with the various squiggly shapes of the words printed in black against white, wondering what they mean. You can recognize your name MELINDA but nothing else. Sometimes you envy Ern for being able to shut himself out in his books during the horrible fights between your parents. You wonder how anyone can learn to recognize so many squiggly shapes on the page and still make sense of it. You think about the signposts outside your house, especially the yellow and red ones. You long to know why cars stop at the red one, and you have been meaning to make a picture of the yellow triangle sign on paper because it has four letters from your name.

The next thing you recall from the closet is Una scooping you up and the soft air from around her throat tickling your ears the next morning. You smiled because it was a pleasant sensation. Una carried you down to the dining room, where you saw Dada. He looked happy in the bright light so you ran to him, just to have him hug you and say you're a good girl after all. You were happy, but you wish he would pat you more often with his hands thick from picking peaches and berries and apples all season. You miss the soft and sweaty warmth that your fingertips always feel when you try to touch his hands as he eats the breakfast Una has cooked for all of you.

But now you hear that sound again: You must hurry or it will go away for a long time. Sometimes sounds you have heard never return, and you are afraid that this will happen with the sound you are hearing. You pull the closet door open, looking quickly up and down for any movement causing the sound. You want to be able to find it; maybe you can make it start whenever you want to. The sound is not clear, but it is a piercing one; you like sounds that pierce because you don't have to strain to hear them. These are the times you feel more like a part of your family.

You close the closet door and walk a few paces to your bedroom. Here the sound registers much more loudly than anywhere else, so you know you've come to the right place. You smile because you know Una is waiting for you or she would not have to keep making that sound over and over again.

You like having Una sleep in the same bed with you. You have been fascinated for days by her growing breasts. Una has tacked color pictures of the fresh-faced teen idols Bobby Sherman and David Cassidy on the wall near her mirror; you know Una would love to marry either one of them someday. She brings homework to her room every night and you always watch her figure out algebraic equations. They have a shape and a line to them that squiggly letters don't have. When Una scratches her head, you know it means she is trying to make her teacher happy. Sometimes you wish you had homework so you could be more like Una, scratching your head in frustration. You are supposed to practice your new sounds for this week, but Una is always so busy. So you are always grateful for just a tired smile from her.

You look over to Dada's bedroom. You notice that some of his clothes are strewn all over the floor, and smell that odor of his. You have known it comes from those Jack Daniels bottles ever since you were allowed to play with one. Then you remember Una's look of shock when she tore it away from your hands. You couldn't decide who was bad, Dada or Una. You had longed to touch the bottle again for a long time until you watched him swallow from it greedily. That was when he turned angry and extinguished his cigarette butts on your bare feet. You screamed from the pain—that was when you learned you could not hear yourself. You don't even remember this at all. But ever since, Una has always watched you in case you want to touch the stinging numbness in your feet. Una also makes sure that you wear shoes all the time, even in the summertime, and that you wear socks to bed every single night. You do all that just to see Una smile, although her smiles are often sad. But you don't care—a smile is a smile.

Yet you feel odd because Dada usually pounds the walls in the kitchen until something falls down. You have never liked kitchens anyway, because you cut your foot once from an overlooked shard of glass two houses before you came to this one. You go into the kitchen only when you have to help Una clean up the table and do the dishes. You wonder now where Dada must be. He must be out of the house. Sometimes when he drinks too many Jack Daniels, he brings different strange women to his bedroom; Una always makes sure that you don't see. But you catch them anyway from your bedroom window when they leave.

You shout gleefully as you push your door open: You see Dada touching Una's breast. Una screams and points to the door, so you run out as fast as you can. You can hear Dada roar in a strange pleasure, his voice mixing in with Una's screams.

You have finally found the sound, and it becomes the first sound you don't want to hear again.

You run quickly down the stairs, your hand barely touching the rail, down to Mama, where she is sleeping from too many pills. You try to prod her awake, but she does not respond. Her mouth merely opens, and nothing comes out but that horrible sound from upstairs.

You run out the front door. You look down and realize you are wearing only socks. You stop, knowing Una would be furious if you were caught outside with socks and no shoes. You think you hear a muffled echo of Una's scream, and you know you must leave. You let the screen door clap shut and run down the street. You head for the store on the corner where that fat man in the dirty white undershirt, Jimmie, always laughs when he gives you a Tootsie Roll for three pennies now and then.

You run in, but he is not smiling now. He bends down to question you, but you cannot lipread him. You are shaking, thinking only of Dada's hand grabbing Una's breast. You babble your best, imitating grownups in school, "Ba ba ba ba!" He puts his hand over his mouth, and then you hear his loud voice traveling toward the back. His wife comes out, and she wipes her floured hands on her print apron as he picks up his telephone receiver and talks into it. His voice sounds very nice. You wish you could do the same thing with your voice.

You stand outside in the hot September evening with Jimmie's wife, who keeps brushing your hair back and looking both ways outside the store until a blue and white car approaches your house four doors away. Soon Dada comes out and shouts at the men in blue. You still want to own a badge like theirs so you can use it against the bad guys, and you begin crying. Dada cannot be a bad guy. You look up at the lady, and you babble angrily, "Ba ba ba ba!" Jimmie's wife nods, and you feel better because she too understands. But she does not do anything except to cover her mouth in horror as Una stumbles out in her terry bathrobe and howls in pain. You catch Ern peeking through the opaque white curtains from his bedroom, and you wave at him. He closes the curtains.

The policemen and Dada are now all sweaty. You wonder how come it is always men who seem to have those wet spots under their arms, and whether it is possible for you to get them too. Finally, one of the policemen goes back to the car and picks up his CB receiver from the dashboard and talks quickly into it. By this time, some of your neighbors have come out behind the police car and windows and fences, all watching Dada's face turning a livid pink. You hide behind Jimmie's wife, afraid that Dada will hurt you once you two are alone in that room. Then you wonder what bad thing Una could possibly have done; you need to know, so you would never make him that angry.

Another police car comes up the street, and then the four policemen struggle to put the handcuffs on Dada. The handcuffs are shiny, reminding you of those detectives on TV. You try to explain to Jimmie's wife that you never meant to cause this much trouble, and she nods solemnly and pulls you closer to herself. As you rest your face in her apron, you brush the flour off your face, because you know if you don't do it, Una will.

You see Mama trying her best to stand, but the best she can do is lean back against the wall next to the front door and make a broken frown. Una tries to help her stay awake as the policemen guide Dada to the backseat of the police car on the right. He glares at you, and you shout back in your best voice, trying to explain that you never thought it would come to this. He turns away, and you look away, knowing that he has never liked the sound of your voice. That is why you never use your voice whenever he starts drinking.

As Dada is driven away, you feel more afraid than ever. You have seen jails on TV and how terrible men in jails are. You don't want to see Dada hurt, and you still can't believe that he is so bad that he has to go to jail. On TV, fathers never go to jail.

You hide behind Jimmie's wife again until you see Una across the street. You don't want to use your voice, but you do. You wave a little and Una opens her arms really wide. You see her white teeth, and you know you have done the right thing. You wonder what Mama will think of all this as you run across the street toward Una. Una slobbers kisses and tears all over you while you babble away excitedly. You notice that the neighbors are clapping so you wave at them. You try to babble your best, explaining that he is not a bad guy. They laugh.

You cannot believe they would laugh at him.

You pull out of Una's arms, and you point at them. Your voice is now loud and shrilly. You keep babbling, and they stop smiling. Una turns your face toward hers, and her eyes scold you into silence.

You turn and notice a neighbor woman guiding Mama back into the living room. You and Una go back to the house. Una says something, and the policemen nod. Then they follow you two in. You look at the blond policeman and how short his crewcut is. You point at it, but Una slaps your hand lightly. He asks, she answers, he writes. She calls toward upstairs, and Ern comes slowly down the steps.

You talk excitedly, trying to explain that Ern was in the next room when it happened. Una puts a finger to her lips, and you stop. You sort of hear Ern's deliberate voice, but you cannot understand him. His face is often a mask. You sit quietly as the day turns into a streetlit night; finally the policemen leave, and Mama begins to sob at last. Una rocks her back and forth. Mama may have to go back to the hospital again.

You remember that place of white corridors. Mama tried to sit upright underneath her white linen sheets when you and Una came in. Mama pointed to some typewritten letters on the small dresser beside her bed. While Mama kept smiling at you, you wondered how she could be sick if she smiled so much. Then you held Una's hand outside the hospital and on the public bus home while you licked a lollipop.

Mama finally dozes off. Una talks nervously with Ern. They both look back at you, and now you know something's going to happen to you. You don't know what it is, but from their looks, they don't like it, but it has to happen. You break into tears that go on forever while Una rocks you back and forth. Finally you fall asleep in Una's arms, almost touching her breasts, without thinking until you remember Dada touching them. You don't want to make any more trouble so you keep your hands to yourself.

The next day a bald man in a three-piece suit with a loosened tie comes to the house. He carries a thick briefcase filled with shiny and metallic things you once saw in a school nurse's office. He's there to examine your feet. You had forgotten all about them. You kick and struggle to keep your socks on, and it takes Una a long time to convince you that it is okay for him to look at your naked feet. You watch him mumbling to Una and scribbling down those squiggly letters in a long and continuous line. He checks his watch now and then as he looks at the rest of your body. You are relieved when he does not give you pain.

Later that day, an older woman and two men come to carry Mama out into a van. You do not say anything because Una is crying, and you know Ern is watching from his bedroom window. You hold Mama's hand, finding it limp, and you look up at Una. She tells the men to get it over with. Una holds you tightly in her arms as the van drives out of sight, and she kisses your face softly. You kiss her back, and you taste the salt of her tears for the first time.

The next morning, your speech therapist comes in and hugs you. Everybody's hugging you all the time now. There are also tears in her eyes, but you do not quite understand why. She hugs you again like Una does whenever she gets emotional. She sits on the living room floor with you and shows you some pictures of a school you have never seen before. She points to it and tries to explain to you that you will be going there tomorrow. You hear Una trying not to sob, and finally she leaves the room. You look around and ask your speech therapist in your best voice, "What's wrong?" She doesn't give you a Froot Loop. You wonder if you haven't made yourself clear enough.

Tomorrow comes. Una tries her best to smile as she helps you put on your favorite dress and fixes up your small suitcase. You talk quietly at first, but when you see a strange car waiting in front of your house, you wonder what will happen to you now. It seems everyone's being taken away, one by one. But Una rides with you, and you feel comforted by her gentle caresses.

Some hours later you see the school in the pictures you saw the day before. As you enter the building, you notice some children your age making strange movements with their hands. You feel angry because they do not talk as well as you can. You point this out, but Una holds you closely. Neither one of you wants to be here. But Una smiles, and you follow her to a dormitory building, and she holds you more tightly than ever before she waves goodbye.

That first week at the Deaf school, you are unable to sleep, and you get faint gray circles under your eyes. You feel proud because Una had them too. You miss her and Ern. As you practice your new signs, you think about Dada, wondering whether you will ever see him again, but you never ask. You don't use your voice ever again, and although you don't like it, you know it's better that way because you don't want to have Una or Ern thrown into jail or into that hospital.

Your memories of that house fade as the language of your new home takes hold in you. You are thrilled that more people can actually understand you when you sign, but you feel hurt when Una visits you less and less often. You know she would never admit that it is still too hard for her to learn your language, or that it hurts her to see you chatting away on the playground with other children, or that you are happier here than in her house.

THE HEALING TOUCH

His shins and calves are dotted with bruises that he will never see; at six years old, he is still learning his way through the house, the front porch, the steps, the crooked sidewalk to the bus stop, the jangling bus where one of his deaf classmates finally puts her hand under his and begins signing. Then another step in front of another step with his unfolded cane tapping lightly in front of his feet: Kids his age haven't yet comprehended the required steadiness of a guide's elbow. He knows the three steps down the bus aisle, the seven steps across the wide sidewalk, and the five steps up before he can walk across the long pavement to the front door. This takes him approximately twenty-eight steps; so much depends on whether a ball or someone cuts in front of him in the rush of playing.

He wears only long-sleeved shirts. He never had to wonder why until recently. He felt a cluster of naked arms in the accidental mob of kids pressing around him against one wall when someone important—teacher? principal? policeman?—was apparently chasing someone. He was never sure what happened, as these kids surrounding him smelled slightly different. He always felt that hearing people did smell differently, but he still hasn't pinpointed why, or how he is able to know whether they are hearing by scent alone. Hearing people seem very reluctant to touch him, as if he is a disease carrier. It will take him a long time to understand why strangers are afraid of him. Even if they claimed they weren't, he is still unable to articulate their palpable fear; only years would explain to him that they felt deep down their very proximity to him just might rob them of their sight and hearing. His long sleeves not only make it easier for others to touch him, but also hide the bruises. They often touch him, forgetting that his arms are still waiting to heal.

His parents are so good, his teacher says. They worry all the time.

He doesn't believe her. Once in the house, where the furniture is never changed, but sometimes bumped or pushed accidentally to the side by his hearing brother's games with his buddies, his parents leave him alone most of the time. They are hardly different from the awkward strangers on the street when they see his perfectly shaped eyelids lifting to reveal eyeballs rolled to the side, so in the house, as in school, he has to wear a pair of dark glasses. Yes, his parents know a few signs, and yes, they do know how to lift his hand and guide it to the plate from which he must eat. He finishes all his meals efficiently and without a word, wondering what they must talk about with their voices. Of course, his parents have never hurt him in any way; they have tried to teach his brother the importance of putting away things. They are just tired of the suppressed gasps of pity from friends and acquaintances. Some of them have decreased the number and length of their visits while watching their children playing with him.

He likes to feel his toys, but he doesn't like braille. Of course, he knows it's a necessity, but he doesn't like reading; most of the textbooks at school are boring. The only good thing about reading is that it means school, a stretch of six hours away from the house where people scarcely touch him unless necessary, as in "bed now." Parched from the hours of waiting to talk with someone in his own home, his fingers at school will be able to cup at last the sweetest water from hands touching back to say, "Me-feel same-you."

REVIVAL

Helene's vision was blurred from the spotlights as she joined her parents onstage before the congregation in the closing shots of *Faith!* one Sunday morning. The show had bought a pair of cochlear implants for Helene, an Akita dog for her brother Bernie, a live-in French chef, and a spacious home on Millionaire's Row. The crowd began singing "Amazing Grace," and she gave a plastic smile while she mouthed the words mechanically.

She prayed Rob would not be the kind to watch TV on Sunday mornings.

The Wynnes headed for their tiny backstage rooms to wash off their makeup. Helene stared in the mirror. She was the tallest girl in her eighth-grade class, and her face always felt oily from pimples that clustered on her chin. Her dull brown hair was parted in the middle; she wasn't allowed to use a curling iron yet. Daddy believed that the iron would get in the way of her cochlear implants. Besides, he wouldn't look very good on TV if he came across as permissive. Helene adjusted her collar; her hair was brushed back, and she scrutinized her pimples one more time to see if they were any less obvious than before. She swept her hair over the cords from her implants. These things made her feel like a freak, and anything she could do to make herself look like anybody else made her feel better.

Satisfied, she turned off the vanity lights.

Helene sat at the head round table in the Brunch Room at the church. She watched her father stand up and smile lovingly at everyone, and her mother smiled broadly, showing off her pearly white teeth, as he gave a speech. She wore a simple wedding ring with no diamond; Jonas Wynne once said on TV, "That was all I could afford those days when I started *Faith!*"

When her mother acted devoted to him, Helene always felt

relief. No more cameras and ribbon-wrapped pocket Bibles till next Sunday. She hated those red ribbons.

Bernie was a fifth-grader and his hair always reminded her of Moe's from The Three Stooges. He had a large dark mole on one side of his neck. She always made sure she sat on his left side so she wouldn't have to see it; sometimes she wondered if Rob felt the same way about her implants. Bernie never said much, but his temper was unpredictable. Their mother would explain on the show how Bernie's temper had taught her so much about the virtue of patience.

But two weeks ago her mother stopped talking about his temper. When that topic came up the last time, Bernie waved his middle finger at a man coughing in the audience. Daddy didn't say a word, but Helene wondered if they had one of those man-to-man talks. Those talks eventually ended up on the show, and Bernie always squirmed.

As food was carted to their table, people passing begged for a word of piecemeal advice from Reverend Jonas Wynne. His hair was thinning and graying, and his glasses seemed liquid along with his expressive brown eyes. His double chin could be seen whenever he was tired from "all that exercise."

As Helene finished her omelet, she watched the action around the large room, packed with the same old people with glazed eyes and phony smiles, and she sighed. She knew how to sigh without anyone noticing, an art in which she excelled.

Her bedroom door locked, Helene tuned in to her favorite radio station, and with forbidden music savored like chocolate mint cookies, she unlocked her diary.

In it were monologues on Rob, a boy whose father taught biology at the university on the other side of the city. Rob wore corduroys every day to school, and he was in half of her classes. She'd never spoken to him, but they knew each other's names from roll calls and whispers from other classmates. "I used to hate school," she once wrote, "until he came along."

His face was embedded in her mind—wire-rimmed thick

glasses, a slightly clefted chin, pale white skin, a blonde crewcut, and peach fuzz.

When dinner was finished, after the cook left, Helene was told to wash the china and the silverware. The suds wore out as the pile lessened. For all their wealth, Reverend Wynne didn't believe in the convenience of automatic dishwashers. She glanced at the clock. It was almost bedtime, when he would walk in.

"It's time to go to bed."

"But, Daddy—"

"Reverend."

"But you asked me to wash these dishes—"

"I can do them myself."

"No, you always have more important work to do—"

His constant smile was a sinister frown and she felt its ice. She threw her latex gloves down and ran upstairs.

She said nothing much as her family's chauffeur drove her toward Evangeline High School. It looked the same as always on Monday—brightly lit windows and dirtied clouds. She took her stance against the fence, watching other kids whose parents had to be better than hers, and waited for Rob to step off his bus. Other than her twice-weekly meetings with her speech therapist, no one paid much attention to her in school. Her parents felt she was completely normal, now that her implants helped her hearing.

In the library, Helene watched Davy sneak up behind Rob while he was drawing pictures of Spiderman in his sketchbook. Suddenly, Davy snatched Rob's pencil and tossed it to his cohort, who then laughingly broke it.

Rob said nothing.

When the school bell rang, Helene handed a pencil to him. She scurried off before he could say a word.

In the hallway of echoes, Rob bumped into her by the lockers the next morning and they looked at each other.

Then she took off for her locker again.

*

When Helene sat down for her lunch in the cafeteria, Rob sat opposite her.

She looked up at him after opening her pudding can, and he smiled clumsily, holding up her pencil with a red ribbon tied around it.

TASTING FIRE

Sometimes Susie would light one match after another, dropping each dead stem into the toilet, like her dad did when he had an occasional gas problem. When he left the bathroom and it was her turn to go, she could discern her dad's gas lurking underneath the ticklish smell of fresh charcoal. Dead matches bobbed in the toilet bowl, and she liked to flush it, just to see them spinning round like tadpoles down the hole. She kept her cochlear implants turned off in the bathroom because she didn't like hearing her mom banging on the door, shouting *please stop playing with those damn matches.* But at fifteen, she was already a junior, and more than old enough to know what she was doing. It was hard to believe that the 1990s had already started.

One night she saw a pair of fire-eaters and sword-swallowers who demonstrated their craft with huge torches and swords on Jay Leno's show. She was amazed that these men hadn't lost the power to speak after swallowing that much fire, and their swords were pulled out without a speck of blood from their throats. She stood before the floor-length mirror in her bedroom and lit a match. She opened her mouth and watched the flame as it went into her mouth. But she breathed too hard, and the flame went out *poof.* She coughed on the paltry taste of smoke clinging to the roof of her palate. The second time, she didn't breathe through her mouth, and the flame flickered less. When she took it out, her hand moved against the ultra-thin transmitter cord that wove around her ear from her implant's microphone to its speech processor box on her waist. The cord pulled down hard, and the top ridge of her ear hurt. She nearly dropped the match on the carpet.

In the bathroom she took off her speech processor and pulled her hair back into a ponytail. She lit another match and watched herself as she held it inside her mouth, daring to close it halfway. The flame felt sweet, almost a tangy bitterness. She nearly gagged on it when she forgot to breathe through her nose. It was a real problem, just concentrating on her breathing alone, because her speech was nasal; most deaf people's speech was nasal if only because they could feel the vibrations of their speech efforts on their throats. She lit one match after another and learned to breathe in the smell of dead matches. She brought the back of her tongue up to her palate. She could taste more of the ashy air. She couldn't stop licking inside her front teeth, making the saliva absorb more of the ticklish taste.

Then in the dining room she brought out a small ladder and climbed it to open the glassed doors of the dining room cabinet where the fine china, crystal glasses, and silverware were kept. She pulled out the box of fireplace matches. Made of wood, the matches were a foot long each, and they had no anti-burn covering. Her mom used them to light the candles in the dining room.

In her bedroom she stared at herself in the mirror above her dresser. She lit a fireplace match and watched its wood stem curl into a charred column that threatened to topple any second. When the fire reached her finger, she blew it out. The chunky ashes were tiny and hot in her hand. She lifted one chunk and put it on her tongue. It didn't taste like what she imagined fire to taste like—just a smoky powder. She took it out and put it on her dresser.

The haunting dream of never speaking again returned. She dreamed of waking up one morning and finding her voice box useless. The world changed because everyone now had to try to understand her in the same way she'd tried to understand them all along. The cruel beauty of forcing everyone to stop pretending that she wasn't quite so deaf—*Susie's deaf? Why, she's as normal as you and me*—was very palatable. She struck the second match against the bottom of the box, held her head as far back as the fire-eaters had, opened her mouth, and shoved the shimmering flame down her throat. She gasped, choked, and pulled it out immediately. She coughed, the insides of her throat searing and singeing; she ran to the bathroom and turned on the faucet for a glass of water. As she gulped the water, she caught sight of herself in the mirror. She didn't look changed or different from before, but the gleam of what she would do for the rest of her life flickered at first, and then shone brightly, in her eyes.

Yes. *Yes.* She would *not* speak. Ever again. She'd learn signs from videotapes and books and anywhere she could, and demand to have a sign language interpreter for her classes—it was the law, after all—and force her speech therapist to learn signs. They'd shake their heads at her obstinacy, soon to be legend. She would stay apart from those hearing people who still treated her like shit, feeling that painful smugness against the fact that it was their turn to learn how to communicate. Every day she would continue to taste this fire, burning alone until that day when she'd find the circus of fire-eaters most appreciative of her craft. She'd speak again, and then the whole world would weep for the fire she lost.

SEALED IN STONE

Fifty years ago, people in town used to whisper about Jeanette O'Connor because it seemed no one wanted to marry her. She was short and almost squat; her body, and especially her forearms and hands, were built almost like a man's. She wore stonemason's overalls that had faded from the whir of grindstone, the brutal chunking-off before carving and engraving a polished slab, the fine powder of granite falling from her stiff sandpaper. She kept her hair short and easy to maintain, and she worked long and hard, alone.

When anyone entered her building next to the Grace River Cemetery, they saw a huge sign that listed clearly the general range of prices, and below it a huge binder filled with headstone designs, typefaces, and icons that the grieving could choose from before writing their names on the receipt, the page number, and, on another piece of paper, the exact spelling of names in CAPITAL LETTERS PLEASE, years of birth and death, and a saying, if any. Then after depositing the 50 percent down payment, they went back to their cars and wept all over again. The fact that she never spoke seemed to appease them more, that they were able to talk freely among themselves without fear of reprisal, that they were able to select the right tombstone design with a peace of mind. While they pored over the much-thumbed binder, she would don her protective glasses and a surgical mask, and get very close to the slab she was working on. Sometimes she sensed their eyes on her as she worked. Of course, there were machines in the shop that could do some things easily, like hacking off top corners so she could create a fat cross on top, but there was no getting around the fact that she didn't have much of the latest time-saving—and very expensive—equipment at hand, so she did what so many others in the business of death had done for centuries: the pain and the monotony of shaping by metal, hammer, and hand for the final farewell.

Jeanette lived in the apartment above her shop, where she'd

grown up; the Grace River Cemetery had been her backyard, where she played and forgot her toys. All during her childhood, she'd longed to have a playmate to play hide-and-seek among the tombstones; there was no better place for such a game. But most parents refused to allow their children to play with Jeanette among the dead as casually as she did. They couldn't get the image of their children's feet stomping on the six feet of dirt above the disintegrating coffins out of their heads. Sometimes Jeanette fell into a deep nap on someone's grave while forget-me-nots tickled her face; there was something intense about studying the work done by stonemasons before her father, and her grandfather.

Mr. O'Connor, her tall and lanky father, complained often of lower back pains from stooping so much to carve and engrave; his work dotted the landscape of the cemetery. He'd learned the craft from his father, and naturally, he was disappointed when his only child turned out to be a girl, and heartbroken when her deafness was diagnosed at two years of age.

Mrs. O'Connor, his red-haired wife, was blessed with a bubbly laugh and arms so thick and warm that she made you want to be hugged again and again. Her earthiness made their customers cotton to her, spilling their tears and regrets while she stroked their backs and shook her head sadly. When she learned of Jeanette's deafness, she wept for fifteen minutes in her husband's arms and then made one phone call after another. Speech therapists came and went, and then finally she drove Jeanette alone downstate to the Deaf residential school.

It was no secret that Mr. O'Connor couldn't communicate very well with his daughter. He didn't believe in sign language, even when it seemed to have brought a shine to Jeanette's eyes. But Mrs. O'Connor borrowed a sign language book from Jeanette's school.

Mr. O'Connor ignored his daughter while she watched him endlessly. She finally took up her first chisel and hammer alone, away from him, at the age of twelve. What she didn't quite know then was that cutting stone is hardly quiet; a relentless rhythm, the wearing down of the human element against nature. As she pounded metal against a chunk of marble discarded the day before, her parents came rushing downstairs; stopped when they saw her master quickly the art of holding the stone at the proper angle for a curve soon turning sensuous under touch. When she was done, her creation looked like a misshapen bowling pin rising out of a jagged chunk.

Her father finally stepped forward, and she looked up. It was the first time she saw him smile, and she saw the rest of her life in that smile. Her mother, laughing with tears in her eyes, embraced her.

Four years later, when her mother died of an aneurysm that pinched her brain dead, her father was too distraught to cut the headstone she deserved; so many visitors spilled out of their apartment and filled the shop and overflowed into the sacred backyard, weeping for the woman they barely knew but loved so much. Jeanette shooed the mourners away, and she stayed up nights and days, bleeding the sweat of loss into stone. Five days later, when she was done, she went upstairs to sleep. The headstone was a stunted column; swirling all around from bottom to top was a curtain of cherubs looking after each other. The name at the bottom on all four sides said MOM.

At first her father wept at the beautiful chaos of loss delineated in those tiny fat arms reaching out yet never quite catching. Then he turned flint angry that she hadn't engraved her mother's full name and years; but because he didn't know signs, he felt helpless to say anything. When the men who usually came on Mondays to haul that week's worth of headstones to their plots arrived, they gasped when they saw the newest one. Her father was moved by how reverently they treated it, wrapping its body in a sheath of blankets before lifting it onto the back of their truck, and carrying it like a trio of pallbearers to its plot next to the Grace River. There, they leveled it ever so carefully; it was like holding a tense child trying to pedal her first bicycle before letting her go. The old boys took off their baseball caps and crossed their hearts for a moment. They had never done that before with the other stones.

When Jeanette came out to the Grace River to see how it looked, there were already some people there, snapping pictures of her very first headstone. Word had already gotten around town. One look at that MOM tombstone, and it seemed that everyone wanted her to do theirs when they died. They said, "Anything you want. Make it beautiful." The trust they placed in her hands sent her searching through the public library for books on architectural and art design—soaring like an eagle, cutting, measuring, redrawing her designs, shaping, sanding. And they wanted the stones placed on their plots before they were dead, so they could see how it would look when they died; only the year of their deaths was left blank. Before long, a well-known photographer heard of her work, came to town, and asked her to point out her stones. When he was about to leave, her father took him aside and demanded that he not mention her deafness in the article. A few months later, when her MOM tombstone was featured on the cover of a Condé Nast travel magazine, the Grace River Cemetery became the unadvertised tourist attraction in a town with nothing else distinguishable about it. Everyone in town whispered about the fact that there was no picture of Jeanette or any mention of her deafness. Finally, the traffic was such that the town was forced to open the cemetery at 8 am and close at 5 pm; it was closed during the burial services. Tourists were naturally outraged when that happened, but they soon saw that if they waited an hour or two, they would have the beauty of peace—and the far-off sobs from the new mourners in the distance—all to themselves.

All this made her father very proud.

Soon Jeanette turned twenty-one. On that day, her father realized that no one had ever suggested a party of some kind in her honor, and that she seemed hardly interested in men. But then again, no man had ever come by to say hello, only because they knew she was deaf. This worried him greatly, as he wanted very much to have a grandson—normal, of course, so he could pass on the finer points of his craft in ways he couldn't with Jeanette, who simply watched and went on with what she chose to learn and show. What's more, who'd want to marry a woman who couldn't speak? No man in his right mind would do that.

He made calls. One by one, the unmarried sons of his friends came and returned with mumbled apologies for blind dates with her that went awry.

She got free meals and saw movies she couldn't quite understand; but then again, those men's action films were so much more fun. Her dates were always relieved when she chose the latest James Bond film instead of a respectful romantic comedy, as might be the case with a hearing date; she often laughed uproariously and unaffectedly at the silliness and preposterousness of the film's action sequences. But there was no chance for them to get her interested in fondling later, in the car. The chemistry just wasn't there.

One afternoon in her shop Jeanette looked up from her work and across the street. She liked having the huge garage door open during the day so air could circulate throughout while she worked. A tall woman with frizzled blond hair and a black outfit with a simple brooch over her heart stood looking at Jeanette from outside the lobby of her apartment building, where most young people just out of college lived until they married and bought houses of their own elsewhere, usually outside the town's limits. It looked like the stranger was dressed for a presentation of some kind, but no, she didn't seem to be waiting for anyone to pick her up. Instead, the stranger was looking at her in that open-faced way that many of her Deaf friends used with each other. She wasn't afraid of making eye contact, like most hearing people; and there she was, a dream with winds of desire buffeting her dress.

At this hour, there was no traffic. The electricity between them as they drew closer jumped like thunder ensnared in a synapse.

In the workshop, Jeanette felt her heart pumping like a sledgehammer pounding against an unshapely stone. She had to touch her neck; she could feel the madness rushing in her jugular vein, as if ready to burst.

The stranger smiled and said something.

Jeanette, not understanding her and not knowing what to say, dropped her chisel without realizing it. She was so—

The noise made them both jump. The stranger laughed nervously; apologized. They both reached down for the chisel, and it was then Jeanette could feel her heat branding her hide as they both lifted and gripped the ice-cold chisel, refusing to let go.

Jeanette guided the stranger into the shadows where she tongued and fondled her so lovingly that she came.

Mr. O'Connor, upon hearing the stranger's moans, stomped loudly on his way down the stairs into the shop. Hearing him, the stranger tried to brush Jeanette's roaming hands away, but it was too late.

The stranger broke away, fleeing the shop, leaving Jeanette aching with a taste for more.

Jeanette's eyes followed her, not caring what her father thought of her now. Mr. O'Connor felt so nauseated that he couldn't say a word. Instead, he went back upstairs, vomited, and tried to sleep.

The next morning, he found it much easier to forget and pretend. He never saw that awful woman again, and he was grateful.

They continued to sit together for meals, but they never looked directly at each other. They had the day's funnies and the news to read at the table.

Jeanette kept a vigil for that stranger from her bedroom window, watching for a sign of her outside the apartment building. She walked up and down the block, peering from a distance into the opened windows for a chance glance. But the stranger never returned. She was probably not even from this neighborhood.

When, one day, a former president of the United States died abruptly of a stroke, she was given a telegram requesting her to create a stone for him. She was completely surprised, for she hadn't cared much for politics, even though the nightly television coverage of politics was always closed-captioned, but it turned out that he, like so many others who came, had seen those magazine pictures and told his wife that he wanted to have his headstone done by her, and her only. Money was no object. Her father wept at the honor and called back a yes at an enormous price. Ten minutes later, it was a done deal. The official letter of agreement stating the price for services to be rendered would be sent via express carrier.

Two days later her father presented to Jeanette the design that the ex-president's widow had in mind. It was squarish and blank-faced, reminiscent of the architecture like that of the famously ugly library named after him; she wanted Jeanette to add her infamous squiggles at the corner and perhaps a whirlwind of cherubs, much rather like the one she'd created for her own mother, on top. No one had ever told Jeanette how to design, and the design was ugly, ugly, ugly! She crumpled the letter and walked away.

Her father shouted rage at her, but she was already going downstairs.

The minute he touched her shoulder to demand why not, she whirled around and spewed forth in sign language, the language she rarely used but remembered vividly from her school days downstate. She was angry that she hadn't been consulted as to whether she wanted the job or not; she would've, of course, but the way he'd gone off, thinking she would do his bidding all this time—no, no more. *Enough.*

He stared blankly, not understanding her at all, just wanting that money, *that money,* the most money they'd ever see for one job in their lives as stonemasons. No pleading on his part could convince her to stop working on the stone for Mrs. Riggs, the one she'd been working on when the telegram came, and in that moment, he wanted to bludgeon his own hands for not knowing her language, secret and obvious and mysterious all at once.

As he typed the letter of regret and sent it out, he wanted so much to choke his daughter, just to make her see that she didn't have to be so deaf and dumb.

Six months later, he died, broken-hearted over the fame that could've been. She did not attend the funeral, and she felt nothing but relief. He hadn't looked her directly in the eye ever since she tossed away that letter; he wouldn't have to do that again. For him, she recreated the ex-president's widow's design from memory, adding a pair of ravens sitting on their perch atop the tombstone. The stone was black, unlike the salmon-colored granite of her mother's tombstone. People shuddered at the pairing of the two—the innocent and the evil—near the Grace River, but her father's stone eventually became one of the most famous, its background story repeated so often that its legend became distorted and misquoted. After all, no one had tried to learn her language. And besides, the more fanciful the legend, the more tourists clamored.

A few weeks later the stranger returned, this time in a jogging outfit.

Jeanette was agape with desire—those tanned legs, those nipples pressing through her exhausted sweaty top, those brown eyes.

They closed the shop for the afternoon, and once upstairs they ravaged each other for the rest of the day. The woman's name was Sara, and she turned out to be newly married with her first child on its way; she'd moved recently to their neighborhood.

They saw each other from Monday through Friday from 4 to 5 p.m., as Sara rearranged her working hours at the university to have an hour of passion before her husband would come home from the Town Comptroller's Office. Jeanette also closed her shop early.

Jeanette felt odd making love to a woman so obviously pregnant, but Sara pleaded with her to explore her further, to make love to her like always, by forcing her hands and tongue all over her body.

When Sara went to the hospital and did not return within a week as promised, Jeanette was hardly surprised. She went on with her work.

A few weeks later, when Jeanette saw Sara carrying her baby into her apartment building. She wept. It was indeed over.

Sara soon left the neighborhood with her husband and baby.

With her father's money, Jeanette bought eight plots' worth of land next to the river, designed and redesigned a blueprint with its precise measurements accounted for, and began cutting the first stone, and then the next. Restless, she designed and shaped each slab of marble into sections that would fit together into a Noah's Ark of sorts, except there weren't any pairs of animals. The boat was filled with naked Deaf women signing, laughing, reaching out to each other, embracing. Their breasts did not have nipples. They were the friends she'd missed so much from her school days downstate. There was only one hearing woman in the ark, and that was Sara; she didn't care how Sara would feel about having her likeness reproduced amidst a subtle orgy of camaraderie.

When she was finished, she hid the slabs and gave her father's lawyers the instructions, which were meticulously drawn, rather like the instruction sheet one got from buying unassembled bookcases. A copy of the instructions was also placed in her safety deposit box in the Lorenz Bank's vault. She couldn't wait to die and be buried inside the most extravagantly beautiful vault ever seen.

Twenty years went by, and Sara never returned.

Only once in those twenty years did Jeanette see Sara, with her children clinging to her, during the Fourth of July parade downtown, but she didn't wave. It was also the first time she saw Sara's balding husband, whose hairy belly protruded disproportionately from the rest of his body.

Instead of making love to the women she desired on the street, and around town, she made love to them in her mind with her supple and expert hands cutting, shaping, nurturing all their sensual qualities out of stone. The Grace River Cemetery was soon transformed into a wonderland of fanciful creatures—sultry cats suggestive of the female body soon became her trademark in a sea of tigers, elephants, dogs, roosters, stallions—frozen in action to contemplate the older stones. No one had ever seen anything like them—*on tombstones!*—

and the most marvelous thing was, people left with a lessened fear of death, even their own.

When Jeanette did die, the town was horrified to see the secret stones she'd hidden from them for so long—*you can't show those deaf ... dykes; why, she's desecrating the dead with that?!?*—and the town council even questioned her father's lawyer on the legality of her instructions. The dispute even reached the national news, and it was the first time everyone learned of her deafness. Elsewhere the Deaf community, too, was ashamed to acquire a posthumous member who had chosen to flaunt her lesbianism in her greatest masterpiece, with all those dancing stones in a cemetery—they never thought a Deaf person would dare do such things.

In the end, when the town's case against Jeanette's lawyer was thrown out of court in the state capital, people relented. Jeanette's body was taken from the town morgue at last and inserted almost unceremoniously into the latch of the ark before it was sealed. The town's new stonemason—hired by the town council not because of his sense of perfection but because he was recommended as being very conservative—couldn't help marveling at the ingenuous tightness of her ambitious design in spite of its themes. Protesters shouting and carrying signs were forced to stay outside the cemetery, and after some teenage vandals spray-painted DYKE FUCK ME GOOD, the town council reluctantly agreed to place the ark under continuous electronic surveillance.

Sara herself was astonished and relieved that no one noticed her likeness, but even then, to play it safe, she demanded to move to another state. Her husband refused. She took their kids and left him for Chicago. No one heard from her again. Soon she was forgotten.

Over the ensuing years, the town gradually shrank, as there were fewer jobs to be had. Jeanette's stonework still drew people from all over the country, and it became the town's singular pride.

Recently, one morning in late November, a pair of joggers who ran daily through the cemetery discovered the body of an old woman with an expensive wig and bright mauve lips, snuggled in a white fur coat under a fresh blanket of snow, curled atop Jeanette's ark.

Amidst a flurry of questions by the police and her distraught children, the dead woman's silence belonged to Jeanette, sealed in stone.

XPT556

On this overcast day in early March, a young woman with her long hair dyed a limp orange gets out of her car in the parking lot. She zips up her lime-green parka jacket and pulls on black gloves. Her boots have spiky heels that stab the crumbly slush on her path into a nondescript building, with its dull brown metal siding punctuated with equally brown one-way windows. It's going to be another day at the Moore Relay Service.

In the cocoon of her cubicle, she is known as XPT556. She has been working as a video relay interpreter for six years straight out of college.

When she was younger, she loved the idea of a secret language that only she and her best friend Pammie Shelton knew. They learned the manual sign language alphabet out of a library book, and they fingerspelled endlessly to each other. They were both eight years old, and Pammie lived down the street. They traded books, CDs, and DVDs, and had many sleepovers at each other's houses. Sometimes they borrowed each other's clothes.

Then she saw her first Deaf person. He was a boy who lived with two older sisters and parents in the newly built house across the street from her. She didn't know that the boy was different until she spotted the bulky earmolds in his ears. Up until that moment he was just another freckled boy with scruffy hair in a blue T-shirt and jeans. He seemed to be about the same age as her.

She was about to say something when her mother whispered sharply, "He's deaf. He doesn't talk at all." They were about to get into the car for the mall.

"Why not?"

The look on her mother's face made it clear that it was not a good question to ask. She wondered why. "Get in the car."

She saw the boy's parents, but she never met them. The father, who wore expensively tailored suits during the day and spotless polo shirts during the evening, was a corporate lawyer who moved his family around the country. The mother, who always wore a fashionable dress unlike most women her age, was a zealously cheerful PTA cheerleader. She saw how she tried to schmooze among her mother's friends at PTA-sponsored events. The mother was such a phony that she was surprised no one had ever called her out on it.

Over the years the boy appeared infrequently, like a ghost. He went to a Deaf residential school so far downstate that he only came up for his winter and summer breaks. He didn't hang out with the neighborhood kids. It was always clear on his face that he preferred to be somewhere else.

His name was Robert McKinder. She loved the sound of his name.

Her first day as a freshman at Linney High School was overwhelming. So many kids, and they all looked like they knew where they were going. But at least Pammie was with her. The two found their homeroom and sat next to each other. They recognized some of their classmates, but due to the consolidation of three high schools that had taken place over the summer, there were a lot of new faces.

She noticed a few people making signs in the hallways. She felt frustrated when she couldn't follow them. "Pammie, look," she said. "They know real sign language!"

That was how they found out their new school offered ASL as a foreign language. Those classes were offered to college-bound juniors and seniors only. She couldn't wait for her turn.

Once, her parents had to leave her alone for a long weekend. They had legally complicated matters to resolve in the hometown where her father had grown up, and he did not get along very well with his many brothers and sisters. Of course, Pammie came over to keep her company.

That Saturday morning she had to feed the three koi fish in their backyard. She liked watching the bright orange-and-white fish dart right up to the pond's surface; she knew that many koi fish could recognize their human feeders. Some of them were willing to accept food directly from their hands; not her father's, though. It wasn't for the lack of trying, however.

When the koi zeroed in on her and waited for her to toss peas and lettuce into the water, she felt a blush of pride. She was special enough to be recognized by fish! Who'd have thought of such a thing when it came to fish?

When hormones began raging through her veins, she cried at the sight of a few blackheads spreading across her forehead and giggled at the budding shape of her breasts. She dreamed about being in love with this or that guy in class.

By the time she celebrated her sixteenth birthday, she had her first boyfriend. She and Mike Clark hung out with their friends in the back of McDonald's on the highway. Alone, they groped each other and tasted each other's tongue in the dark of his souped-up Corvette. Mike was an okay varsity basketball player, but he was a great kisser. She loved the feel of his smooth shoulders when he took off his shirt. But she knew that no matter how much she wanted him, she wasn't ready to have sex with him. He had to wait.

They talked about getting married.

The names for their four kids. Two boys and two girls, alternating every other year.

The kind of house they'd buy.

The kind of high-paying job he would get. He wanted to be an auto mechanic. He worked on cars for his father's friends who were into collecting vintage cars.

Then six months later, Mike admitted to having fallen in love with someone else. He didn't say who.

Crushed, she sulked for days afterwards; she didn't want to talk to anyone at all. Not even Pammie. She moped when she walked the hallways between classes. Her parents had to bribe her with a used 50cc scooter that was repainted in pink just for her. She was apprehensive at first, but the minute she strapped on her matching pink helmet and throttled her bike, she was off and running.

The barren spaciousness of the countryside beyond the city appealed to her. It was nothing like the houses in her hilly neighborhood. Houses there seemed perched together as if they were a flock of birds. Their backyards were big enough for koi ponds and gas barbecues. And there were a lot of fences.

Even though there were miles and miles of corn and wheat

starting to grow, the countryside felt uncluttered. She felt as if she could scoot straight upward to the heavens and fly like the geese already flying north in their V-formations to their summer breeding grounds.

Then Pammie got pregnant and had to put the baby up for adoption. That was how she learned that Pammie had been Mike's "mysterious new girlfriend" all along, and that he was the father. It was the first time in her life that she understood why people who loved each other dearly could turn against each other in a single flash. She vowed never to talk to Pammie ever again.

With Robert McKinder gone to school, she took to looking out for Pammie down the street and turning her face away whenever her ex-best friend happened to glance her way. Though she knew it was totally wrong of her to do so, she took a particular pleasure in watching Pammie's pregnancy transform her into a blimp.

Pammie had always been a slender girl, but impending motherhood seemed to add slabs of fat to her hips. A few months later, her size was startling.

She swore to herself that she'd never get pregnant. How could anyone look like that and still be attractive? Even Mike seemed to wince a bit when he leaned over to kiss her on the cheek in front of Pammie's house.

When she heard that Mike had left Pammie for someone else, she felt a huge load fall off her shoulders. By then Pammie had become an outcast. No matter how hard Pammie tried, she couldn't seem to regain her previous figure. Pammie sat alone in the cafeteria.

It would be a few years before she ran into Pammie at the mall. "My God," Pammie said. "You look great, and I look like shit."

"Sorry. What?" She was surprised that she hadn't recognized her ex-best friend at first. Pammie wore too much mascara, her flat hair looked stringy, and her winter coat looked like a bloated smock. Her own mind had been abuzz with the Christmas gifts she had to get for her parents. She was on her winter break from college.

"I deserved what I got after what I did to you."

They hugged and made promises to make it up to each other. But it wasn't the same. They had long discarded the ghost selves of their shared girlhood, and strangers had taken their places.

*

By the end of her first week of ASL classes in her junior year of high school, she knew what she wanted to be: an ASL interpreter. She was fascinated by the style and beauty of her teacher's signing. She felt like an utter doofus when she tried to copy the teacher's smooth signing.

But she didn't know then that to learn ASL properly, one had to turn off her voice. Ms. Toni Anderson, who was hearing, had managed to get hired at the high school even though she had only two years of experience with ASL, with some church interpreting experience, and claimed to know a number of Deaf people in the city. In class, Ms. Anderson rarely admonished her students for using their voices while signing.

She wouldn't have known that a number of Ms. Anderson's students, thinking that they were fluent enough in ASL since Ms. Anderson had told them so, met with these Deaf people only to find that they'd never thought well of Ms. Anderson's incorrectly formed signs and found her presumptuous attitude deeply offensive. Eventually a few Deaf people showed up at the principal's office and complained. Ms. Anderson was fired, and a Deaf instructor replaced her.

She didn't know then that many hearing administrators in high schools had often felt so intimidated by the notion of sign language that they were too afraid to hire Deaf instructors. The sound of a perfectly modulated voice was always the song of relief after having used ASL interpreters in interviews, not to mention the unnecessary expense of having to hire them for meetings every now and then.

She didn't know then that ASL and English never mixed well, especially when using one's voice at the same time. Or that ASL didn't follow the syntax and grammar of English.

But who cared about such things at sixteen? She was in love with the way her hands could be so full of *meaning*.

Some days when she practiced her signing in front of the mirror, she imagined herself becoming translucent like an angel. Her wings would glitter like a mist of diamonds that fluttered majestically when she lifted herself upward. People were wrong when they said the Holy Bible was the Word of God. Right there in her hands was the truer

Word of God. How could anyone not see that? By then she was taking her second year in ASL.

She wanted so much to be fluent enough to explain all these things to Robert each time she saw him come and go from his house. As much as she wanted to, she didn't dare cross the street to him.

She dreamed of appearing like a shimmering vision in his bedroom. Her hands would create perfectly sculpted signs to create a simple message of comfort and grace: "You may not believe it, but God is everywhere with you." He would smile and forgive her—and every hearing person—for everything.

The phone rings. She leans forward in her chair and presses the accept button. Each time she does this is always a test. The stranger on the videophone will observe how she signs and fingerspells her interpreter ID number, and in a few seconds just how fluent in ASL she is and whether the rhythms of her signing have been tainted by using Signing Exact English before learning ASL. She knows enough to wear solid-colored tops for better contrast with her hands, and she always removes jangly earrings and flashy necklaces before she starts her interpreting work.

She waits for the screen to reveal her first client of the day. She can see herself in the upper-right corner of the screen. She looks good. Nearby are other interpreters in their own cubicles, talking with hearing callers through their headsets and signing to their Deaf clients on the videophone. Sometimes, when a call is put on interminable hold, she puts up a privacy screen. She tends to do this when she doesn't want to have an off-the-record chat with the Deaf client while waiting for the hearing caller to return to the phone. She hates it when a man wants to ask her out for dinner even though he has no idea which city she lives in. It would be a breach of confidentiality to share personal contact information.

Right before her appears a slender man in a white T-shirt and knee-holed jeans. He is sitting on one end of a low-slung sofa that looks like a cast-off artifact from the 1960s. Behind him is a hallway. His long hair is pulled back into a ponytail, and his sideburns are bushy. The floor lamp next to him emphasizes the paleness of his forearms. The tattoos on his biceps look like shadows that keep reappearing.

Right below the screen is his name and city: Robert McKinder from Marquette, Michigan.

After learning the rudimentary basics of ASL in high school years before, she couldn't wait for Robert McKinder to come home so she could practice her new skills with him. Every day she looked out the front windows of her house for a sign of him.

Then her father slipped on a patch of ice on the first day of her Christmas vacation. He had to be put in a body cast. His spinal cord was out of whack. She had to get up early every morning after snowfall and operate the snowblower to clear the driveway.

One morning she caught sight of Robert snowblowing his parents' driveway. She walked across the street, took her gloves off, and signed with her voice, "Hi! I'm learning ASL. I think sign language is so cool! Can you understand me?"

He gave her a look that said, *You think you know ASL? Oh, please.*

She felt as if her knees would collapse. She hadn't expected such a rude response. She'd thought that all Deaf people would be very happy to see a hearing person so interested in their language. After all, not enough people know ASL, right?

She didn't know then that Deaf people were just like hearing people. They were like a big family filled with histories of feuds started and forgiven. That they still looked out for each other regardless was testimony to the tribal power of language inherent in their hands.

She blinked her eyes, not knowing what to do. Her tears began to trickle and freeze.

He took off his gloves and signed, "Sorry."

She lit up. "I know that one!" She didn't sign.

He mouthed along with his signs. "You same-same hearing people who want-want learn A-S-L. You think nothing fun signing cute-cute. Stop. D-o-n-t don't learn A-S-L with attitude a-t-t-i-t-u-d-e attitude. R-e-s-p-e-c-t where?"

She nodded meekly and didn't use her voice. "Sorry."

The rest of her Christmas break felt long and dreary with overcast skies. She still looked out the front windows, but it wasn't with the same intensity as before.

She began borrowing books from the public library and reading up on the history of Deaf people and their education. It was then that she'd understood his anger. Hearing educators had literally tried to banish ASL because it wasn't a spoken language. She read horror stories of how they tied Deaf children's hands behind their backs in the mistaken belief that if they couldn't communicate with their hands, they'd learn to speak instead. Sometimes they struck their signing hands in the classroom with a sharp ruler, not realizing how much hatred they would inspire among those who felt liberated in the clarity of communication.

She felt worse than before and resolved to change her attitude when she returned to school a few days later.

In the safety of her cubicle, she searches the man's face to see if it is indeed the same boy she once knew. Nonetheless, she knows she must stay cool, professional. She had worked very hard to earn her Registry of Interpreters for the Deaf certification, but she knows she isn't skilled enough to interpret spoken poetry and stage play productions, the toughest kind of spoken language of all to translate into ASL. She feels utterly hopeless when it comes to translating a poetic line like "Stars are burning in the velvet blanket of my heart" into ASL. Should she sign "heart" first, then "same" "blanket black v-e-l-v-e-t" when the poet likens the blanket to a night sky? And how should she sign "burning" when stars twinkled? But if she signed "burning," wouldn't the blanket burn as well? She liked the sound of that line, but she knew her limitations as an interpreter. She needed to study ASL interpreters far more skilled than herself to improve.

She signs, "Me number XPT556. Call who please?"

He signs, "E-v-e-l-y-n Evelyn."

"Call now." She presses the dial button and adjusts her headset.

As she waits for the mysterious Evelyn to pick up the receiver, she looks at him again. She wants to ask, "You before live where B-e-l-k-i-n Street around ten years ago?"

The phone rings. She counts the number of rings with her hand.

He nods in understanding.

She keeps trying not to stare at him. Is it truly him? Or was Robert McKinder a common-enough name? She had thought that her name was unique enough until she googled it one day and found to her dismay that there were four other women with her name living in the same city.

The phone picks up on the fifth ring. "Hello." A woman's voice. She can't quite place her age.

"Is this Evelyn?"

"Yes. Who's this?"

"Hi. This is XPT556 calling from Moore Relay Service. Have you used video relay service before?"

"Yes. Is this Bob?"

She looks at him and voices his signs as he gives a hesitant smile. "Yes. That's me, the one and only."

"Oh, good. I was starting to worry when you didn't call me back yesterday." She translates what Evelyn said into "Good. Me worry you-call-me not yesterday." She knows it's not ASL enough, but he seems to be following her.

"A lot's been going on in my life. Okay?" She knows her proper English translation pales to his rangy ASL, which is so full of emotion, colored with apology and rage.

After high school she moved to Monmouth, Oregon, for a collegiate four-year program in ASL interpreting.

She learned how to remember what she'd just heard so she could repeat in signs. It wasn't easy at first. She froze the first few times. The fear of being judged critically had paralyzed her, but when she saw how others still fingerspelled clumsily when she kept her fingerspelling hand in the same spot, she knew she had an advantage.

She thought of dating a Deaf man. There weren't any Deaf students at her college, which was odd given that there were so many ASL interpreting students. Most Deaf people lived an hour's drive north in Portland, and they rarely came down to Monmouth.

Every Friday night she joined some of her classmates at a coffeehouse in Portland where Deaf people socialized. She sat quietly on the sidelines and watched. She wanted to tell her friends to stop using their voices with their hands, but she didn't want to be a spoilsport.

She lit on a man who looked to be in his mid-20s. He looked like a former football coach, and his hands were full of vigor. He wore a baseball cap and a light jacket. He looked like he was talking about bowling with an older buddy of his, but she wasn't sure.

Then he caught sight of her gawking. His face said, *What are you looking at?*

She blushed and turned away. When she finally gathered up enough nerve to look his way, he'd shifted his shoulders away to block her view of his signing.

"Bob? Bob? Hello?"

Evelyn's voice snaps her out of her reverie. "Sorry," she says. "Can you repeat that, please?"

"Bob, you're not the only one with problems. Everybody's got problems." She translates that into "You think you only-one problem-problem? Everyone-out-there same you."

"You're calling about Dad, right?"

"He's back in the hospital again. The doctor says he doesn't have long to live. Your father wants to see you."

In that moment she realizes that Evelyn is Robert's mother. She wonders if Mrs. McKinder is still wearing stylish dresses at her age, or if she looks something like Barbara Bush, all jowly with pearls.

"Never. And you want to know why? You never learned my language. You expect me to come home immediately whenever Dad gets sick, but do you come here when I get sick? No. You just don't want to use your hands because it's too much work. Have you ever thought about how much work it takes me to make my speech clear enough for you?"

"Bob. I'm too old to learn sign language. I've got arthritis in my hands."

"You're so good with your excuses I'm surprised you haven't won an Oscar."

"Please. Your father has a few days left to live, so please come down here and say goodbye to him."

He stares at the interpreter a moment. "So? I'm not coming."

"Why the hell not?"

"Why should I come home if you never listened to me in the first place?"

She is relieved when Evelyn doesn't respond right away. She catches the sound of tears welling up in Evelyn's throat.

In the summer between her junior and senior years the McKinders put their house up for sale. The red-and-white sign with its phone number and house ID number gleamed in the sun. It was a matter of weeks before the word SOLD was pasted on the sign. She didn't see him or his parents again.

She wondered for a long time where he'd gone. She compared every Deaf person she met against Robert and saw how unique each Deaf person was. They didn't sign or speak the same way. It took her a long time to differentiate the many regional dialects used among ASL signers, and that's where being a video relay interpreter helped. Callers from all over the country used signs she'd never seen before. She had to learn them quickly.

After graduating from college and returning home, she dreamed of accidentally bumping into Robert, now a full-grown man, and showing him how fluent she was in his language. She wouldn't hold herself high and mighty like some of her friends in college had. She wouldn't be flashy with her signs so he'd know that she was respectful of his language. She'd be accepted into the Deaf community.

The sound of Evelyn blowing her nose into a tissue awakens her from her daydream. "Sorry. I needed to clear up my nose. You still there, Bob?"

"Yes." He looks warily at the interpreter.

"What I want to know is why you moved to Marquette. There are no jobs up there. Why do you have to make it so hard on yourself by moving so far away from us?"

He rolls his eyes. "You still don't get it?" He inhales. "You know what? I'm still not coming to the hospital or his funeral. You two are not my real family. You never learned ASL; therefore that means you never wanted me, period. Stop wasting my time. Goodbye." He makes the sign for "phone hang-up finish."

"Wait—"

"Want phone hang-up anyway?" She asks him.

"Yes."

"I'm sorry, but he's hung up already." She speaks to Evelyn and signs to him.

"Can't you call him back? Right now?"

"You'll need to dial from your own phone. I'm sorry."

She hangs up and looks at him. "True-biz sorry you-two parents problem. Hope situation dissolve soon."

He shook his head. "Doubt-doubt. Thank-you interpret-interpret."

"Welcome." She glances back through the gap of her cubicle to see if her supervisor is monitoring her. "Quick question. You before live B-e-l-k-i-n Street?"

"Yes. Why? Who you?"

"Me before live across street your house."

His face lights up. "Wow-wow. You same girl who mangled-mouth signs?"

She smiles. "Yes. Me think improve some."

"Wow." He applauds. "Me proud you. Deaf people nitpick you signing, but you suffer-suffer through pah. Me proud you."

"Thank-you." She hears a peculiar warning sound. Interpreters are not supposed to chat long after each call. "Sorry, but hang-up must. Supervisor watch will. Bye."

"Wait!—"

The screen turns black and lights up again, this time to an overweight woman with a squalling baby on her lap. The glare of a fluorescent light glares at her from the left. Not ideal lighting, but she's seen worse. She signs, "Me number XPT556. Call who please?"

Later that night she dreams of shimmering like a fiery koi fish pushing upstream inside the telephone lines from her home to his place in Marquette, Michigan. Her hands would be full of sparkling electricity, and he would tell her stories he'd never tell another hearing person. And she'd tell him how he had saved her at a time of dark reckoning. No longer XPT556, she would become a real human being with a first, middle, and last name, and with a history worth learning, and he would remember her as much as she had remembered him.

NEIGHBORS

[in ASL gloss]

House-house-house that-way neighbors new move-there. These-two move i-n eight-nine months ago, not sure exact when, eight-nine-months approximately. First meet, me-think okay-okay. Both hearing, facial-expression-extreme-show-teeth-for-lipreading not, nice. Themselves dress-fancy not. Man pants s-w-e-a-t-pants purple, T-shirt purple same, but strange what? Gold thick-elaborate-surround-neck b-l-i-n-g. Himself brag show money have. Me-look-him-up-down, okay. Other-person woman dress same-same j-u-s-t different color but unique what? Simple necklace gold p-e-a-r-l pendant. Odd man dress-loud attract-attention-from-everyone, woman simple good-enough. Their preferences respect okay.

Two-cars parked front have. One old blue paint fall-off-here-there r-u-s-t thick-layer bad whew. Other car strange: car fancy-fancy B-M-W hot red, black stripes-emanating-from-front-grille-lining-car's-side, thick wheels. B-M-W typical-typical car not. Car expensive obvious whew-whew. Car strange worse what? My area you-know: nice simple houses, good school nearby, kids play all-over safe, neighbors down-the-block windows watch-supervise kids play. Live here thumbs-up. Plus neighbors here-there sign fingerspell a-bit, better than nothing. Fine-fine accept all-right.

Before explain deep happen, me-backtrack explain happen before these-two move. That house before own who? N-o-r-m-a-n S-l-i-m-m, name-sign-NS, nice old man. Like work-work fix-fix house, mow-mow, house clean-perfect pow-chin whew. Me-admit jealous house upkeep whew, but okay. House mine clean-clean perfect not, accept. NS hearing, not sign, but write-back-and-forth problem none. Us-two get-along fine. One day himself fall sudden front house. Me-spot-bam run-fast gently-turn-him-onto-back, himself-breath-hard, me-text 9-1-1 "heart-attack come now." Me-know 9-1-1 point-find-me fast. Me-focus NS careful-careful all-right, me worried okay, not sure, but watch-watch anyway. NS try talk, but lipread hard why? Part-face frozen, me-realize s-t-r-o-k-e. Me watch-watch look-around ambulance arrive, wait-wait, me worry. Pah! Ambulance arrive. Me-step-back let m-e-d-i-c-s do-do-do business theirs. One woman approach-me not realize me-deaf, first confused. Me-phone show type back-and-forth, question-question-me, type-phone work-out okay. NS carried-away hospital. Week later come-home. Walk slow, different. Part face stiff. Facial-expression odd why? Left-eyebrow up-down-movement none. Blink can, but look-me strange. Time progress, me-used stiff-eyebrow. Write-back-and-forth same before. Stroke effect not bad. Me relief. Back-then house clean-perfect, now what? Little-by-little house clean-perfect dissolve dirty. Me-offer clean-clean house. Me good neighbor want. Agree, okay-okay. Weekend me-come wash-floor, wash windows, carry-machine-weed-eater-around house-base, trees back. Me finish thumbs-up me-go, but NS come-come, gesture money. Me no-no. Me-acquiesce meet-him garage. He-write, You good neighbor, best. Wish more neighbors same you. Wish you my son.

Heart-touch. Me-gesture thank-you.

That night true-biz heart-attack die.

Couple recent move house his? Man NS son that. Different father wow. Background story not-know, but obvious flashy attention-want. First think money earn how? D-r-u-g-s. Week-week later eye-spot fancy car park front house. Money where from? Not obsess, but let-it-go. Plus busy j-o-b kids house upkeep et-cetera, pay-attention those-two not. Busy-busy.

But one thing notice: man fancy bling drive car fancy, woman simple drive car old. Strange, hit-me, oh-oh: why man support woman money none? Old car that replace need. Man money give-give buy new car, why not? Not make sense.

S-o: me decide watch-watch out-of-the-corners-of-my-eyes what's-up-what's-up these-two. Me do-do, like drive school drop-off kids, me go work, me food shopping, et-cetera. Me come-go come-go. Me set time follow strict not. First take-care-take-care family home.

Anyway, yesterday strange happen.

Me happen mow-mow l-a-w-n morning. Hot sweat nose-wow but problem. Rain-rain recent all-week grass too-tall. S-u-n fine grab opportunity mow-mow. Know-that-know-that rain tomorrow do-do, have t-o mow-mow. Go-ahead mow-mow. G-a-s run-out. Nose-ptooey. Mow 1/2 finish. Plan go garage me-spot-bam woman three-places-down sit p-a-t-i-o cry-cry. Look-like blood head but can't t-e-l-l three-houses-down, plus sun-in-my-eyes. Me-stop do-do? True-biz beat-up? If call police, find nothing, laughter-caught-in-throat? Me-go ask help? No interpret. Hearing you-know emotional cry-cry hands-cover-face lipread how?

But still me-doubt, help, hands-off?

Woman head turn-quick, man walk p-a-t-i-o. Bling gone. Appearance ordinary. Tank-top shorts finish. Those-two mouth-talk sudden argue-argue yell-yell. Man point-finger woman, woman point-toward-me. Not think those-two see me there. Argue-argue awful. Me-think leave alone, go-ahead garage g-a-s container bring mower. Pour g-a-s finish, put b-a-c-k finish. Me-pull-pull-start mower. Old, you know? Have t-o pull-pull whew, but run good. Dad give-me his old still-standing real-fine. Motor run perfect. Me go-ahead mow-mow, glance those-two argue still? Seem they-left, okay. Mow-mow finish. Me sweat stink nose-whew, time shower. Ready enter bathroom shower, front-door-lights-flash. F-k! R-o-b-e put-on-me, walk-down-stairs open-door. Woman p-e-a-r-l pendant stood there. Face shoulder arms blood b-r-u-i-s-e. Me-think, Communicate how? No paper write-back-and-forth, no phone type-back-and-forth. Me gesture, Wait-one-minute. Ready enter house get paper p-e-n, but woman do-do? Sign. Mind-me enter house? Her-sign not awkward, not like hearing, you-know? Fluent sign like deaf. Mind-flipped. Herself not come house inform-me sign before. Anyway, woman-stand there signing. Happen herself C-O-D-A grow-up parents deaf. Few years back herself enter program d-e-t-o-x why? Drug addict. Hard work become clean, d-r-u-g-s, alcohol, marijuana all stop. During program met NS son same problem. Both fall-in-love, but s-e-x none because program forbid.

Man true-biz work-work quit d-r-u-g-s, but problem: sober few months, w-a-g-o-n fall-off, roller-coaster. Woman frustrated, not-know do-do. Seem that morning those-two argue why? Man beat-beat h-e-r. Took car k-e-y-s, I-D, et-cetera, escape can't. I-D out-there important, you know? Woman fed-up decide come-straight-me house why? NS tell-her me deaf good neighbor. Mind-scar that. Me-suggest call police file report catch-him bring-to-jail, maybe herself go special house women D-V. Et-cetera that. Woman sweet why? Call police request interpret if need me witness. Nice whew. Police come those-two house. Woman hide my house, policewoman know where hide, policewoman interpreter slip-undercover my house back door, police interrogate woman then me. Paperwork fill-out finish, police car arrive these-two house. Police knock-knock, man open-door shock yell-yell, swear look-like, turn-around take-off, but police capture-him arrest handcuffs finish. Stay jail how long, me not know, but important everyone safe.

WINTERLOVE

We always came home from school together. Her house was one block over, so we played together year-round. Most of our classmates never played together in the summer. I felt lucky. My younger sisters always nagged me to go plait their hair and play with them, but even at thirteen, I felt too grown-up for them. Besides, I liked my brand-new hearing aids, and the earmolds were colored brown, just like my skin. They were the kind I'd always wanted—behind-the-ear—ever since I was little and had to wear those hearing aids on my chest. I felt so free.

My speech therapist pointed out that my "Cherry" sometimes came out like "chewy," so she suggested that I call my best friend by her real name instead. Cheryl's skin was like dark honey, her hair was nappy in a don't-mess-with-me way, her eyes were brown and shiny as chocolate chips just out of the oven. She showed me her breasts once, to show me how developed she was. I wanted to touch them, but I showed mine instead. I was flat-chested, but she didn't look long, even when I left it open longer than I should. She simply laughed. She said that flat-chested girls have it easier in the world. I wanted her to go on and explain, but by then, she'd finished buttoning her blouse. "Too cold in here," she said.

I knew I was okay because *Newsweek* did a cover story on people like me. My parents were subscribers, and they didn't seem to mind the two women posed on the cover. In my bedroom, I left the magazine out where Cheryl could see it. I wanted to ask her what she thought of the cover, but she was already pulling out our history textbooks. We had a quiz to study for, and this time it was about the ancient Greeks. I knew about Sappho, but there was no mention of her, or I'd have copied her revered fragments on torn pieces of paper and leave them strewn about for Cheryl to find. It was only a matter of time.

After all, it was the 1990s.

Along came Will Smith, swaggering right into her dreams. He was the guy who'd saved our planet twice in the movies *Independence Day* and *Men in Black*. Cheryl said, "Oh, but he's soooo cute!" She plastered posters and pictures of him all over the walls of her bedroom that winter; she even started to wear lipstick because his girlfriend used it too. We spent two hours once after school comparing the dark reds against the color his future wife Jada Pinkett used in a picture in the *National Enquirer*. But we couldn't agree. I let her win.

Another time she brought her videotape of *Bad Boys* over because our TV had a built-in closed-caption decoder. I'd never seen that one, so we plopped down in front of the TV with our buttery microwave popcorn. The smell of butter overwhelmed me. I had the distinct desire to put my arm around her, just to sniff the perfume of her adoring eyes never leaving Will Smith. I simply moved my hips closer to hers. She didn't move closer. I licked the buttery residue of popcorn off my fingers instead.

One night, after school and two weeks before Christmas vacation, I touched her face and blurted, "I love you." I couldn't help myself. She froze, then thawed enough to put her boots on and leave. From my bedroom window, the December snow had an ashy pallor. She didn't even turn around and wave goodbye like she usually did.

In the clangorous corridors of lockers opening and banging shut, she avoided me in the weeks that followed. I spent more and more time with my Deaf friends, and I stopped using my voice. Christmas came and went, and on New Year's Eve, I climbed out to the backyard and watched the stars while resting on my back. When I turned off my hearing aids, the stars seemed to come into an incredible focus. I dreamed of being the first Deaf astronaut, zipping away faster than the speed of sound to the barren red lands of Mars. Cheryl would be so sorry that she turned me away.

One Saturday I brought my younger sisters along with me to Lake Luna where a threadbare blanket of snow had fallen on the ice. In the shack there, with a fireplace going at full crackle and roar, we changed from boots to ice skates. My sisters squealed with almost every klutzy step they took. Sometimes I had to pull them up and show them again how to skate, how their ankles had to remain strong for balance. Finally, when they were able to go ten yards without falling, I felt gloriously free, skating forward and backward as needed to keep a constant eye on my younger sisters. Then without realizing it, I went *vloom* past Cheryl and her new friends, who glued on their long nails and curled their hair so much that it reminded me of those little plastic canisters for 35mm film. I imagined myself as the first Deaf black figure skater with the most gold medals at the Olympics. I paid Cheryl no mind, and then on my third spin around the lake, I slid past the orange cones that warned of thin ice. The surface went *humph* under me. The astonishing slap and choke of gray water gurgled around my body as I let myself fall into the gaping hole of fury. Its chill was the most beautiful warmth in the whole world, and her screaming for someone to come pull me out made it all the sweeter. When a stranger dragged me out an eternity later, I was shivery and feverish with love.

HOW TO BECOME A BACKSTABBER

1. Discover the value of your own deafness.

This is not as easy as it sounds. If you are deaf, many people—including some Deaf people themselves—think that you shouldn't limit yourself by solely communicating through signs, and that if you have sufficient hearing, you should use speech whenever possible. This depends on your background, of course. You, for example, were born hearing, but you lost most of your hearing at the age of four due to rubella. You are the second daughter, and the only deaf person, in your family.

You are told that sign language is bad, so you have to watch your hands carefully. You hold your hands together when you daydream in mainstreamed classes, or when you speak. You enjoy speech lessons immensely because it means getting attention. You don't mind the repetitive drills of consonants and vowels, and the pronunciation of words you've never heard before.

One day, though, your life is forever changed. You meet Bill, a second Deaf student, who is actually hard of hearing but spent most of his education in a Deaf school recently closed by the state, and who uses sign language. You are fascinated in spite of your speech therapist's constant admonitions; you feel funny when she tries to force Bill's signing hands down on the table. You look at your own hands, wondering.

Those high school days are wonderful because of the clandestine language. You have mixed feelings when your hearing classmates come up to you and say, "Marlee Matlin's so amazing," or "Heather Whitestone's inspiring." You don't dare admit that you can't understand Matlin's signing at all, or that you feel funny about Whitestone's implied opinion of oralism being far superior to sign language. You are constantly badgered by hearing classmates on whether you know the sign for this or that, and your opinions on this or that Deaf person in the media, but you don't dare come out of the closet. You have nightmares in which your hands are chopped off and your tongue is anointed with holy speech.

Your speech therapist asks you daily whether you've learned any signs from Bill. You shake your head no. Everyone you know adores your speech, but Bill much prefers your hands. But everything is so easy, easy to say with hands, and easy to tell on his hands whether the signs are clearly enunciated—the inestimable beauty of hearing with one's eyes.

2. Spend a great deal of time with your Deaf friends.

In a hearing college 200 miles away from home, you connect with some Deaf students. You discover a world of language, culture, and friendship. High school is a dim memory, and you no longer remember why you'd once had such a huge crush on this or that hearing boy. Bill, your first Deaf friend, is now at Gallaudet University. You can't imagine going away to a school hundreds and hundreds of miles away, and going there without even checking it out first. But that's what he did. He had been so unhappy with all those hearing classmates in high school, and he'd wanted to quit and find any old job anywhere. You are still relieved that he stuck it out, and that he actually sent you a postcard from Gallaudet, as promised. He wrote, NO MORE HEARIES. HAPPY HAPPY HAPPY!!!

In your dorm room you stare at the postcard for a long time and tack it on the bulletin board above your desk. *Happy? Him happy?* It is hard to imagine him that way, really. He was always so pissed off at the world, especially at the state legislators who decided his Deaf school wasn't worth the expense and shut it down for good. The state's debts, compounded by a limp economy, had grown too large to ignore. You vow to visit Gallaudet one day.

Your Deaf friends at college tell you stories from their lives, and you begin to feel warmly whole. At home you still speak, and you don't tell your parents that you're using ASL out in the open at school. You are eternally grateful that they're paying your tuition, but you know they'll never understand you as you are. The very idea of you using ASL would break their hearts. After all, they've donated a great deal of money to the Alexander Graham Bell Association over the years and are often listed prominently in *The Volta Review*.

Yet their love for you can't be mistaken for paternalism. They've genuinely tried to encourage you to participate in various extracurricular activities at school, and they do attend as your devoted cheerleaders. You love them because no one else cheered for you when you came in next-to-last in women's track, or when your science project won third place. You were never told that you couldn't achieve anything because you were deaf. But the unspoken corollary was that sign language would hinder you in insidious ways.

But those stories told by your Deaf friends enrage you. They were unjustly punished merely for wanting to communicate clearly, even if it meant through their hands. You vow never to let that happen again, and you take out your Alexander Graham Bell membership card and light it with a friend's match. They clap with glee, and you know you've found a better home than your parents could possibly imagine for you.

3. Ignore the little insecurities that nag at your Deaf pride.

After graduation, you move to Seattle. You find a job as a computer technician; you had been surprised by how much fun it was to fix those damn things in college, and now you can't believe that you actually get paid to do such things. Of course, the fact that you are both female and Deaf seems to bother some of your clients, but they say nothing when they observe your troubleshooting speed. *Boom-boom-boom*. You're out the door, and your clients are already raving about you to their friends.

You still talk with your parents through email.

In time, you meet a cute Deaf man named George. You fall for him because of the way he signs, in a slow-pokey kind of way. He is a computer programmer, but he is such a child at heart. He plays games all the time, he thinks nothing of wrestling with buddies in the living room, and he has a big heart. He comes from a Deaf-strong family, and you are struck by how included you feel in his family. They welcome you with open arms; they are so relieved to see that you're indeed Deaf. Just like them. They don't have to justify their ways to you. You and George become engaged.

When your parents meet George for the first time, they turn quiet with rage. They don't say anything about his gravelly voice or bad speech, but they are not forthcoming with hugs or attempts to be close, as they were with your hearing sister's boyfriend—now her husband. That day, out of eyeshot, George turns to you and says, "Hearing control wedding not-want."

You compromise with two weddings, the first one taking place in a Deaf church. On the day that you marry, your parents weep, unable to communicate with those who clearly care for you; your sister keeps smiling as if nothing is wrong. You send interpreters their way, but they're too frightened to make conversation with anyone. They can't stop watching how George and his pals carry on as if they never left school; in fact, you envy their shared past and their tight-knittedness. Your parents cannot disguise their discomfort, even with your second wedding in their church where you always sat in the third row to be able to lipread the minister.

With your husband, you find yourself more and more drawn into the Deaf community. He reminds you not to pay any attention to the gossip swirling around you: Dave makes nearly twice what you make, and he's only two years out of college! You saw his paycheck. Mina has married a hearing man who can't sign for shit, and she comes from a Deaf-strong family! Scott, a heavy-set oralist, brings his thin hearing lover to a particularly rowdy night at the Deaf bowling club! The guy has a tan so dark that his peroxided hair looks white. You see him carrying on like a sissy in front of all those beer-toting straight bowlers. And worse yet, that bitch who stole your best friend's husband now claims to have known your boss all her life!

George reminds you not to pay attention to all of this.

You repeat the grumbly things he has said about this or that pal of his.

He rolls his eyes as if to say, *They're just Deaf, okay?*

But it is not long before you serve gossip along with toast in the morning, constantly comparing yourselves with these people.

4. Spend so much time with your Deaf friends that you practically *have* to start talking about each other. (A corollary: The smaller the community, the better.)

With the birth of your first baby, you suddenly feel the overwhelming presence of Deaf in-laws peeking out of the shadows, wondering whether your Eileen is hearing or not. A month later she is found to be deaf, and there is so much jubilation on George's face that he breaks into tears. You decide to stay home for a year or two, then longer when you learn of your second pregnancy. Your next baby, Robert, is hearing. You put your job on hold.

With both children you and George never use your voices. You simply sign, almost forcibly teaching your children signs instead of speech. Their eyes light up when they see you signing to them. They can't stop grasping for your fingers. You are so full of love, so full of hugs for them at every turn, that even George has to chuckle. You two no longer talk about other people, but about what's best for your beautiful, *beautiful* babies. At home, you feel at peace, more so when George plays with the children trying to climb up the moving mountain of their father in the living room.

Sometimes some of your Deaf friends who are also mothers visit with their kids, which is always great. Naturally, everyone talks about babies, but you suddenly feel a little out of it when they start discussing Al, one of your husband's best pals. Seems that he's been having an affair with a Deaf high school senior girl, and his wife, Betty, hasn't talked to him ever since she found out.

You don't know Al very well, even though he's the one who's always there whenever George needs help with moving huge furniture around, or building the back porch, or painting all the walls upstairs in your new house. You've never sat down and talked with him as a person, not as someone who's known your husband all his life. You like him, though, because he is clearly a good man, a citadel of reliability, and someone who seems incapable of dishonesty. Before you'd heard all of this about Al, you wouldn't have used the word "seems." Everyone, you thought, really liked him.

You bring up the story with George later that night.

"What tell you before?" He explodes. "Not true! Not true!"

Nevertheless, you vow to keep an eye peeled for any telling detail.

5. Pretend to be concerned in front of the people involved.

At a social party held for local alumni from the National Technical Institute for the Deaf—your husband George had earned his bachelor's in computer science there—you run into Al's wife. You are pleasantly surprised to find that she doesn't seem embittered at all. Betty comes up to you and asks how things are.

You share the latest on your babies. Eileen is now walking and climbing like crazy, and she has to be fenced in no matter what. Robert is obsessed with eating asparagus, dipped in mayonnaise. Betty laughs at the image of your boy dipping and flipping the mayo all over the kitchen floor before eating the stalk.

Finally, you broach the subject. "How you?"

She doesn't let on whether she knows that you probably know. "Fine A-l work tonight." Of course. He works the graveyard shift at a Microsoft factory, keeping an eye on its security. It's a tough job because so many software packages slip out the back door and end up sold on the streets of New York and elsewhere, way below wholesale, and the guards often get the heat for it. You remember how Al had explained all of this to you one night, when you were all a great crowd who always got together every weekend to party. That was a long time before any babies were born.

She smiles and says nothing more.

You glance around the room, full of people whose faces you know, and most of whom you've gotten acquainted with here and there through various Deaf social functions over the years. You turn to Betty. "Me sorry."

Her face turns a little hard. "Gossip stupid."

"Stories true?"

"Play dumb you? For-for?"

A mutual friend enters the room with her husband, and Betty is gone, waving hello. You turn and catch Michelle's knowing glance; she's married to one of George's pals. Seems you weren't the first to ask Betty tonight.

6. Instead of feeling hurt, wear your feelings on the outside.

For days afterwards you can't stop wondering whether your trustworthiness has become devalued among your friends, and whether they've been talking badly about you. You've been in the

Deaf community long enough to see how some Deafies can easily spread inaccurate and hurtful stories, if only to destroy the ones they don't like. Often, when you and George talk about throwing a party at your house, you two have to write down the list of all the guests and see if you know of any bad blood among any of them. Sometimes it gets too complicated, and the party almost never happens. But it finally does.

One day, some friends come over for coffee and bring their kids. Once they're satisfied that their kids are safe in your childproofed backyard, they share the latest soap opera installments on this or that Deaf person you all know either by sight or by acquaintance. Somehow, without thinking, you pry loose some deep-down opinions. George's always warned you of sharing your innermost thoughts with people you think are friends, but these days he seems constantly weary; at his company, the project of migrating from Windows 98 to a whole new—and invariably better—operating system has become much bigger than anticipated, what with bugs in the hardware and politics within George's department. Completely attentive, the friends are suddenly yours. Their appetite for what you think of others seems insatiable. They nod agreement, and when it's time for them to leave, you know you've hit on something. You're not sure what it is, but you like the sensation of feeling this intense kinship with them.

7. Warning: Someone will backstab you sooner or later. (Usually sooner.)

You are buckling the kids into their booster seats in the back of the car when you catch George giving a slight wave to a beautiful blonde strutting by to the supermarket behind you. You know he didn't think you'd catch that, but you have sharp eyes. Ever since these friends keep coming back for your thoughts, you've become much more aware of how men behave among themselves and among women who are not their wives.

You sit down in the car. "Saw you."

"Me do-do?"

"Girl over-there you wave."

"Looked-at-me smile."

"Smile wrong?" He turns the ignition key and says nothing.

When you are all home, and the food has been put away, he turns to you. "Heard many-many stories about you. Friends some-them don't-want visit come over any more. Sick-you gossip."

Usually the loquacious one, you feel unable to say anything.

8. Above all, deny that you've ever said a bad word or spread rumors about anyone.

That night you snuggle up to George. You lick his sweet back slowly, in the way he'd said turned him on, but tonight he doesn't respond. You know you've lost something, something that these friends of yours wouldn't understand. You sigh, thinking instead about your kids, and how much they need a father in today's darkening world.

In time, he will probably have affairs with other Deaf women, who usually outnumber Deaf men by a wide margin; no wonder that Deaf wives can be extremely jealous of single Deaf women. In time, George will extend more of his love on your kids; of course, he still loves you and talks with you and all that, but it's not the same. And in time, some of his pals will return to watch sports on his huge TV, if only because they missed his company. But you'll always be remembered as someone who'd neglected the vigilance of watching her own hands.

MY MARTYRDOM '06

The day will soon come when your Deaf community and culture as you know it become an object of curiosity on the wall. Too many successful Deaf people have gotten the hearing media's attention, mainly because they have refused to feel discouraged by the backstabbing within your community. Too many legislators have gotten the impression that, like those in the news, you're capable of being integrated with the hearing world, so they go ahead and close your Deaf residential schools. Too many Deaf people are realizing that they don't always need their own community to survive, to be true to themselves in what they do. Sure, they have questions about their own identities, but they are already looking for answers elsewhere. Don't you see what's coming? Oh, come on.

The Great Deaf American Dream is falling apart big time, splintering your community into a million directions like never before. No one agrees on anything. Compromise suddenly seems like a mortal sin. Each group has become more and more an isolationist foreign country. You read about each other, but you never invite each other to dinner, just to be friends in a world that once punished you for your inability to hear. The "them" is no longer strictly hearing; "them" has become Deaf too. I don't like it, either.

I had a GPA of 3.91 in American History from Hunter College, but after graduating, I disappeared into the crowds. I'd seen too much underneath the surface of your community. I didn't want to go on for a master's degree because the academia was not the best place to evoke much-needed social change within your Deaf community. Besides, it broke my heart to see every Deaf person I knew taking sides on this or that issue without even listening to each other.

One night, at a Deaf club down in Brooklyn, I saw some of these people that my friend mentioned, the ones who I thought were friends but who backstabbed me when I wasn't around. I waved hello to them, but not once did they come over to ask how I was doing. It seemed like I had been ousted from their midst. What had I done? Just because my signing ability isn't that fluent? Just because I sign and speak at the same time? Just because I'm a woman? Just because I have rich hearing parents? Just because I earned my B.A. in three years instead of four? Just because I'm bisexual? Just because I kept questioning everything about Deaf culture? Just because I kept wondering out loud: What the hell does "not Deaf enough" mean?

I had to get out. You know how to dole out pain with your tiny glances, the swiftness of your hands. Someone must've taught you well.

But no more cruelty. Enough is enough.

That's why, at this precarious time in our communal history, I chose to peddle the worthless banknotes of your language. To drag you back to where you started in the beginning, to remind you how much work you have to do before other Deaf people with so much potential can pull all of you out of your stupid fox trenches. Deafness is a beautiful trinket chest that never stops gushing forth objects of both beauty and stupidity, pride and shame, and dignity and confrontation. You know what else I think? Deafness may not be a disability, but your infighting definitely is.

Every day, in Manhattan, I carry my backpack loaded with the pastel-colored cards showing the alphabet, and work the subways, keeping a hawk's eye out for cops and plainclothesmen. I can sniff them out easily by the way they hold their eyes and hands, a simpleton's language to translate. In the rare instances when I'm arrested, they hear my garbled voice and observe my patience instead of blowing my top like some other Deaf peddlers who insist on too much innocence, and they always let me go. The other peddlers hate me because I'm clearly better educated and have better speech. See what I mean? No one wants to work together.

At night, deep in the heart of Arthur Avenue, the remaining outpost of an old Italian neighborhood in the Bronx, I watch TV and write. I have an old DOS computer that I found in a trash bin that still works, and with it I think out loud on the screen about the history and the future of your people already in danger of extinction. Sure, I'm no Charlton Heston who can part the Red Sea to the Promised Land of happiness for all Deafies, but that's because you're too busy squabbling over this or that. I fear that when all you Napoleons finally stop, whether it be from exhaustion or old age, you'll see how your forces have thinned in your absence. That's the real tragedy, more than who's right and wrong in all the controversies followed by *Deaf Life* and *SIGNews* and online at deafread.com. In politics, numbers do count, and your infighting hasn't helped anyone at all. There is no community in the Deaf community. You're making it easier for the hearing world to dismiss you, just when they are trying to figure out how to give you a place at the table.

Maybe I'm being egotistical when I say I want to become a textbook example of a Deaf person who has so much potential, but the Deaf community martyred her instead. Oops—another potential Deafie leader with brains bites the dust. Yes, I'm still bitter. Anger hurts in every sign I make. Oh, I know I'm no saint, but neither are any of you. No one is. After all this time of learning your language, you've sentenced me to a purgatory of loving your language and being unable to use it among you.

These days I keep to myself and maintain a journal of my peddling and the various customers' reactions, and my observations and reactions to books on deafness I borrow from the public library. But it's already a book that no one will care to read. Too many Deafies are away from home, at war, unwilling to face the future when there'll be so few of us left that we'll have no choice but to accept each other as we are. Until then, I'll continue to peddle and pray.

AN AFTERNOON WITH JOAN JETT

Plug me in and crank me up, baby. I got my shirt and tight jeans on right, I got my air guitar waiting for me, I got fresh batteries for my hearing aids. My dad and mom are gone for the afternoon at some crappy wedding for a business friend's daughter, so that means I get to rock and roll alone to that stereo cranked way up loud in the living room. I put my favorite Joan Jett album into the CD player and turn the speakers face down on the floor. I love the way the rhythm booms through my bones whenever I prance about with my air guitar, just like Joan Jett when she's slinging her guitar on stage with that angry pout of hers.

Joan Jett doesn't know it yet, but I play guitar better than Eddie Van Halen or even Jimi Hendrix. I'm gonna be huge and sell a lotta copies like her. I'll have a million fans obsessed with *me*, and they don't care that I used to be a wallflower dyke who surfed the web at night, chatting with women who never knew that I'm hearing-impaired. It's spooky sometimes how much I know about rock and roll. God, I'm so tired of explaining my stupid hearing aids to everyone all the time and offending anyone when I tell them I don't know sign language. What's so bad about that? I don't know any other Deaf people around here. Sure, they're out there by the hundreds on the web, but I don't need sign language to talk with them. We both got keyboards to talk, and that's enough.

Right now I just want to shout out loud to the world how much I love rock and roll, and I'm not talking about the sanitized crap that's on VH-1. *Yeaahhhhhh!!!!* I love the way Joan's voice goes—*ohhhhhh*—right there near the end of this song. It's like she's making love with me, except that she's not; she's asking me if I wanna touch her (*oh yeah!*). I don't know if it's true that she's one of the family, but I don't care. I just love the way she plays off the frets. I jump about and swing my windmill arm to make a piercing twang on my guitar, just like Pete Townshend. I prance around the coffee table as if it's just another piece of band equipment and then leap onto the sofa before our screaming fans. I yell along with Joan: "Yayyyyyyyy! Oh, yaayyyyyyy!" My voice gives out, but I got to show who's still got the best groove going—no time to give up now. I point with a grin to this or that girl in the audience who's got the sweating hots for me; I can see their eyes as they reach out as one big organism with only one thing on their minds—to touch me—but the cops are holding them back. I catch myself in the hallway mirror, wiping my dripping brow, and I see dark puddles sliding down my clothes. "Do you wanna touch me?" I sing. I got to show 'em how hot I'm getting for those sexy girls lunging forward and moving to *my* music. *Whoo*-ooo! Look at 'em dancing so close—you can tell what's gonna happen tonight. "Oh, yeah!"

The song ends in a fadeout. I'm left with my hearing aids squealing feedback. I turn the volume down until the feedback stops and slump onto the sofa. I feel great. I try a "Yayyyyy." It comes out wispy-sounding. The stuff of legend, I'm not. I'm just a homely fifteen-year-old hearing-impaired flat-chested dyke who hasn't had her first fan yet. There are several kids in my high school who are gay, but they're all hearing boys who get beaten up at least once a week. Sometimes I get so angry about that, but I can't say anything. I don't want to be the only dyke out there; besides, my parents would freak out if I told them, just like Ellen Morgan's, except that her parents are a little too dumb for me. There are a few girls at school who I suspect are like me, but they don't have the nerve to say anything either.

Maybe tonight I will fake my way into one of those bars I've read so much about on the web—I know there's got to be at least one for dykes somewhere in this town of 50,000—and see my own Joan Jett leaning against the bar, her mascara-heavy eyes devouring me and her leather-clad hips showing me how my hearing aids and wispy voice don't matter at all next to the real fine bad reputation she's got waiting for me.

EULA

It's been a long time since I said anything to her after the accident when I died. She was always the kind of daughter that I dreamed about when I was a little deaf girl lost in the babble of my hearing family's conversations. She would be intelligent and witty. She would be sad when she cried. She would be silly when she laughed. And she would sign, and we would understand each other perfectly.

I had three hearing daughters before Eula came along. I wept with joy when I learned she turned out to be deaf. She was adorable and sweet when she was a baby, although she had a heart problem that prevented her from playing as much as my other girls. She had those cute freckles sprinkled so lightly over her cherubic face.

But when I see Eula now, I feel a strange kind of sadness. She finds herself unable to feel beyond grief because of me. She's trying to cope with my absence after so long, after eight years. I feel sad that she hasn't experienced the shattering pangs of falling in love yet, and that she's hiding herself from herself. She's twenty-one now. Hard to believe she's become an adult already.

I want to reach out to her and say that I'm all right. I want to lay down with her and hug her like I used to do when she was scared in the hospital before heart surgery. But this time doctors can't help her. She has to be the one to call the moves on her heart, not them. She has to decide what's next before she is prepared for the first cut into her mind and soul.

I am so proud of her successes at my alma mater, Gallaudet. I have many warm memories of the college way back in the early '60s when it was slowly expanding. Of course, that was when I met Erik Larsson from Minnesota. I could say that it was the first time that I ever really fell in love with any one man. I've never regretted marrying Erik because I have had such wonderful girls, especially Eula. I miss Eula the most when I watch her go through the motions of everyday life at Gallaudet.

There are so many bits and pieces of advice that I want to share with her, but as with all things in life, there's never enough time. I never wanted to die, but Fate beckoned me. My death was really peaceful: I woke up walking to the end of that long tunnel, following that calm light. I remember telling Erik, who had tried to follow me into the light, my last words: "Go-back. Girls need you." I was scared that the girls would have to suffer more from having both of their parents die in a silly American dream car that spun twice in the air, tossing all of my girls out on the wheat fields, before it landed on me in the ditch. But I'm glad that he survived the accident. I still love him madly, although he's married someone else partly to help take care of the girls.

Even though she's the youngest, Eula seems so much older than the rest of my girls. I keep thinking of that anger bottled inside her, and how much older it made her in such a short time. She's had to grow up faster than the rest just to survive my death. I can understand part of her anger over the fact that my family didn't send her for counseling the way they sent Elise almost immediately after my death; Eula needed as much help as her oldest sister had. Elise was my first baby. All the mistakes that I made were on her, but she's made it through okay. I'm so happy that she's married with three kids. It's so frustrating because I see rapid changes happening within my girls and in the world out there. I may be behind the times, but I'm never far behind with Eula.

I want so much for her to live her life to the fullest. I don't care if she falls for a woman. Doesn't matter to me as long as she's happy But she's got to stop letting my death control her life. She needs to be really free, the way she was those few weeks after her successful heart surgery: She could finally run and play like the rest of the kids. I'll never forget her expression of freedom while she played and played all day. I want to see that expression on her face again.

When she finally does, I'll let go. Until then I'll keep signing to her every morning when she awakens in a fog of prayer: "You wings already have. Go-ahead free fly."

for Willa

GAMES

There's a picture of me from the Christmas of 1975. It shows me sitting in the kitchen, on the bench between the table and the large window, and I am putting some Lego bricks together. If you look at it closely, you'll see my old hearing aids. I wore them on my chest, almost like a bra. My hair looks a bit ragged, but it's still a dirty blond. In fact, my hair appears more yellow than the dull kitchen walls. I am wearing an acrylic blue-and-white turtleneck sweater; all my hearing brothers and sisters were too busy playing with my oldest sister Gracey's new hamster Homer to pose for the photo. I was nine years old at the time.

Gracey took that picture without warning. She had been using her new Kodak camera all day. After that happened, I rubbed my eyes to get rid of the ping of the flash imprinted on the insides of my eyelids. Then I went on with my Lego building.

Even when I try to forget that bright silver-gray flash, I try to recall how Gracey looked. She was a little heavy around the hips and she wore those bell-bottom jeans with platform shoes. She parted her brown bangs with hairpins and let the rest of her hair fall back in a neat, straight line. Sometimes she'd strut around the kitchen and giggle at how swishy it all felt.

But Gracey was Gracey. Because of her job at Marty's, a highway diner in my hometown of Olney, she could afford the latest fashions, unlike anyone else in the family. She was always far-out and groovy and peace-brothers-and-sisters; those were the words in her handwriting on the box of her favorite game, Twister, and on her album cover of Elton John's *Goodbye Yellow Brick Road*. I remember these words clearly because she had gotten her colored pens the same day she brought home that record.

Gordy must've been twelve at that time. His reddish-brown hair came up thick and coarse; the only way to fix it was to keep trimming it short. His teeth were a little odd: Each tooth appeared not to touch each other. We weren't that close, but to my nine-year-old mind, he must've been the next thing to Peter Pan. I envied his ability to leap without looking.

One Friday night we made a game of our own. We called it Watch Out and the gameboard was created using Gracey's Bic Banana magic marker colors. We must've drawn at least one hundred arrows that inevitably said, "Sorry! Go to the JAIL because you're too cheap!" all over the cardboard and played it at least a dozen times before we turned in.

As I lay beside Gordy on our double-sized bed, I imagined us being the penny and the nickel on the gameboard; we'd be fighting for our own lives and trying to make the best of what the dice spelled out for each other. In the end he'd always win; but because I was his brother, I was allowed to live.

It was an unusually warm day in May when Frankie came home from the hospital for the first time. I thought to myself, *I don't want a new brother*. He seemed too pink and passive, awash in his sunshine-heated cotton blankets whenever I peered at him through the big crib in Mom's bedroom. How could he play with me? I was five.

A few years later I was playing with my Tonka trucks when Mom slowly walked a few paces behind Frankie as he wobbled onto the porch. He waved at me, smiling. I gave him a *What-are-you-doing-here?* look and went back to my trucks.

Then I heard the sharp punctuation of Mom's voice in my hearing aids. "Michael, don't ever do that again. You're his example and you don't want him to be like Gordy, do you?" She bent down and gave one of my trucks to Frankie. "Now, you two share and share alike."

The winter of 1975 was a cold one. I'd put on my long underwear and slipped my brown terry socks over them. Sometimes I'd put on some wool socks, too, but I had to be careful of how I put them over my first socks because I never liked the itchy touch of wool. Then I'd slide on my J. C. Penney's stretch jeans and my favorite red-blue-and-creme argyle long-sleeved shirt. I'd put on my khaki green parka jacket and zip it all the way up to my nose. I'd put on my ski hat, the kind that looked like a house when it was flattened in the hallway bookcase near the side door. I'd be wearing my hearing aids, and I always felt the pressure of my earmolds painfully whenever I pulled my hat down on them.

I'd then let Gracey tie up my snowmobile boots. I'd wiggle my big toes, and she would feel for them. When she got them, she would open her arms, and I'd rub my nose into her soft shoulder. She would open the door as she tucked in the bottoms of my double mittens; she would make me blow my nose one last time before going out. After twitching my nose a bit, I felt ready to brave the new cold world.

I ran gleefully, kicking around the snow crystals, all the way around the house to the backyard. I'd look up to see if anyone was watching me from the windows. When I saw someone, I'd wave.

Most of the time it was Gracey who'd wave back.

In the back seat where I rode for two hours every Sunday night to Lansel, where I learned how to speak with other deaf children also brought together from the area, I kept my head tilted backward so I could look up at the stars, twinkling amidst the blues and grays. I imagined myself stretching my dragonfly wings wide and coasting on the wind with my eyes closed from my hometown to Lansel. I had done this for almost as long as I could remember.

During the week, when I stayed with Mr. and Mrs. Carter, my foster parents, I imagined them to be a family-in-waiting. They both worked full time at Lansel State University. I knew their routines, but my guest room was a temporary place full of dreams that they never pinned to the wall.

Through each speech lesson in Lansel I kept thinking of home, anticipating each Friday afternoon when I'd return to Olney. I always flew home with my eyes wide open, chasing the glorious sun west.

Sometimes I'd play with Frankie, who was now five, in the snow. He was shorter than me and his cheeks were really pink; his baby fat hadn't left him yet. His mousy hair and lips were thin; his eyes seemed to beg for attention like Winnie the Pooh's Eeyore. But he rarely complained as he helped push the increasingly heavy snowball while making trails all over the side yard; it'd take us a few hours to make such a snowman. There is a picture of us and the snowman, but the background—our blanketed hill—was so white that we looked like shadows in it.

I always felt uncomfortable with Frankie; I felt obliged to order him around. He was the only one who didn't try to tinker with my hearing aids when I took them off at night before bed.

Before Marty visited us that Christmas to give Gracey that hamster, I never had much experience with pets. We had just gotten Judy the October before, and she had mushroomed into a huge German shepherd.

Judy was an excitable dog. If I clapped and barked "Giddap!" she'd jump suddenly out of her nap and begin running back and forth through the first floor of our house. She'd jolt from Mom and Dad's bedroom in the rear, through the hallway and the kitchen, toward the living room where she'd leap at and bounce off the back of our sofa before running back. Every one of us soon learned how to make her run for some bits of hardened bread. She loved to chew them and left behind some crumbs that stuck between one's toes if one didn't watch where one's bare feet went.

My younger sister Aimee must've had her eighth birthday the month before Homer died. At that time I envied her because she had her own Etch A Sketch and I didn't have one. It was also a gift from Marty.

I had always thought of her as a big blabbermouth, with capital B's. I did play with her, but I didn't quite trust her braided blonde hair or her *I'm-always-innocent* blue eyes. Her lips were thick whenever she pouted, which she seemed to do often.

The night when Homer died, my second-oldest brother Ethan had just finished assembling his fourth World War II plane from a kit. Its empty box became Homer's coffin.

I remember how light and heavy it felt. Over and over again I kept reading the white graphic letters on one corner NO GLUE NEEDED until I felt numb, even when Gracey read some lines from the book *How to Cope with the Death of a Loved One* from our local library.

We stood like fat bears around the tiny hole we had dug and its adjacent pile of extremely hard and brittle soil. Two shovels—one already bent from breaking the dirt—were staked in the snow a few yards away.

I also remember the look on Mom's face. I thought she was trying her best not to cry, but if I remember detachedly, it must've been her trying not to laugh. We had just used up two boxes of Puffs wrapping up Homer for burial.

Two summers before Marty gave her Homer, Gracey decided she would build a go-cart. From the back of our garage, I helped gather up an old neglected door with peeling paint that revealed both pastel pink and blue underneath. Then I followed her into the Ace Hardware Store downtown as she bought corrugated fasteners. It took her all Saturday to put the red bike trainer wheels under the door and tie the front wheels to a huge and blistery rope loop. When she was finished, it was five o'clock.

Our house stood atop a hill. It wasn't steep, but it was easy to cruise our wagons down if we wanted a noisy ride with muscle-straining steers around the four potholes at the bottom. As Gordy rode up the hill with his buddy Steve and his mother from their day at Olney Lake, his eyes turned a bright agate blue as I clutched on to Gracey from behind with her crazy laughs echoing in my hearing aids. Glenna, my second-oldest sister, snapped black-and-white pictures with her camera. We still have those pictures somewhere.

As I pulled the go-cart up the hill, Gordy gave us a sullen look, one that meant he was going to outdo Gracey.

The next morning as we prepared for Mass, Dad heard Judy the dog's whimpering and he told me to go bring her inside the house. As I unleashed the dog, I caught Gordy's *What-do-you-think-you-are-doing-here?* look as he hammered together his first go-cart. By the time we came out for our ride to church, he had tried out Gracey's go-cart to see how he could make his better. It was not long before Gordy and Gracey competed all day to make one for each one of us—all of us including Mom and Dad. When Gordy asked Dad for the bottom half of our screen door so Judy could have one, he said, "No." Years later Dad would say, "I never seen those blasted doors disappear so fast and Gordy wasn't in shop class yet!" It was one of Dad's favorite stories about us growing up.

His vivacious eyes are what I remember the most about Homer the hamster. He was decidedly similar to Judy except that he loved to run the wheel all night long in the cage. It used to drive us nuts at first when we'd walk up to his cage and he'd sleep through our yelling, "Good morning, Homer!"

When I touched his amber-and-white fur, I couldn't really feel his coat, as if he never existed, a crystallization of my imagination. But I could feel his whiskers and the nasty pinch from his tiny teeth whenever he was in a cranky mood.

Even then I loved to play with him when no one else was around. I'd open the cage and beckon Homer to come onto my palm. He'd clamber up, knowing this could be his opportunity to escape. But I was always careful. I'd make a circle with my index finger and thumb—it was not much bigger than a quarter—and let Homer slip through. It always amazed me that this incredibly fat creature could wriggle through a hole less than one-third of his size. I called this exercise a "slipthrough." I never tired of it, but when Homer began to twitch around, I knew I had to move fast. He usually peed on my hand when I dropped him onto the floor of his cage. It was an inevitable mess: droppings on some face of a SUNDAY COMIX cartoon character, wet spots on some Dow-Jones indices, and tiny pieces of nibbled paper.

In the living room Homer's cage sat on a makeshift bedside table by the front window where an antique Seth Thomas clock tick-tick-tick-tick-tocked every five seconds. After his all-nighter Homer would hide and sleep all morning like a smudged cotton ball inside an orange plastic hollow ball. I won that toy orange from a game at the St. Rosita's Halloween party the October before. Judy never took to it, so I gave it to Gracey and she left it on her dresser until she got Homer.

I also liked to watch him suck greedily from his upside-down water bottle so I could watch the water bubble a little while his eyes pierced me. I thought he was mad at me for watching him so closely. After all I hated it too when Aimee watched me eat cookies.

After Homer died, I put on my rubber boots and pushed the clasps over my Oxford shoes when the snow melted. I also put on my hat and parka and mittens.

The backyard was muddy, but I could detect the distinctive odor of spring. It didn't smell of decay and decomposition; new shoots of green appeared amidst the yellowed grasses. It was in the middle of April when I went out to check Homer's burial site.

I saw its clumsy oval and knew that its grass would look different from the rest of the backyard's.

One August night years later, I tried to pinpoint it. I couldn't.

The day when Homer died, Gracey was taking a nap, as she had to work the Friday night shift at Marty's. She was upstairs when I decided to take Homer out for a few slipthroughs. I had to play with him, just for a minute, even if Aimee was there. She was struggling to fit an orange blouse on her Barbie doll at the other end of the living room.

So when she heard the click of the cage door, she opened her mouth to say something—I put my finger to my mouth. Her eyes were wide open as Homer slipped through my circle a few times when Gordy sauntered in with a *Casper the Friendly Ghost* comic book.

She turned her head and screamed.

Gordy dropped his book and hollered at me. I turned to get the cage door open in time, but it was too late. He lunged at Homer, still sniffling around in my hand.

"Gimme it," Gordy said.

"No," I said.

"GIMME IT."

"NO!" I turned around and held Homer to my chest as Gordy pounded on my back. I fell down, but I got up just as quickly. Aimee screamed again when Gordy clutched one of my shoulders and pulled me around. His lips were tight as he pulled Homer from my hands.

"There, you got to be responsible," he said. But as he petted it, he looked down. Homer was already dead.

He looked up at me. When everybody else came running in, he put Homer back into my hands and pointed at me. I looked wildly at everybody while Gracey opened my hands.

She articulated carefully, "What happened?"

I stumbled for the right words, but Aimee's excited voice cut through my nasal haze. "He didn't do it, honest. I saw the whole thing!" I wanted to hug her.

*

The house was very quiet that night as I lay on my bed upstairs, with a bedside lamp and my new library book, when Frankie climbed up the stairs in his thick snowpants and navy-blue suspenders. He tugged at my shirt.

"What do you want?"

"Everybody's outside. They're looking for a place to bury Homer. Wanna come out and help?" His eyes pleaded, *Don't let me down again.* I glanced away; then I closed my book slowly and followed him downstairs.

SOMEONE ELSE'S FATHER

The boy is about to pinch his nose before plunging underwater to play "Shark" in the shallows of Willow Lake when he notices the sun bouncing off the rippling of a man's bare back in the shimmery distance. He doesn't hear his younger brother or anyone call his name; his body hearing aids are nestled in the roll of his Dr. Pepper beach towel. He is ten, and he is spending the summer once again with his family.

He doesn't know the man's name. It's always too hard to make out anyone's lips when it comes to new names; his family is used to scrambling around for a piece of paper and a pencil to spell them out. He'd like to know the man's name; he's seen him before. He is perhaps a Whirlpool repairman around the area; his build is stocky with firm pectorals. The boy wishes he was allowed to wade out that far. He watches the man's muscles rippling and quaking as he bends down to twirl his arms in the waist-high waters. His shiny back looks speckled with freckles, with the beginning of slight love handles above his trunks. Two boys are darting around him, chasing each other.

His younger brother sweeps an arc of water with his arm. "Shark! Look!"

Closing his eyes, the boy pinches his nose and feels in the cool shallowness for his younger brother's skinny legs.

After a while, the boy tires of playing "Shark," and he looks around to see where the man has gone. The man is napping on his stomach on the shore. His body looks silent, hardly aquiver with a breathing life.

Later that afternoon, the boy has changed into the dry comfort of his clothes, and he sits, eating potato chips near his family's picnic table under the trees. His mother is in the girls' building where she is changing his younger brother, as he's only four. He watches his two older brothers still swimming and calling to each other off the shore.

They are shadows lost in the glimmer of floating diamonds.

His father is sitting at the other end of the table, reading a Western pulp novel. He looks up at his son with eyes that try to smile.

The boy wonders again if it has anything to do with his hearing aids, and he remembers how his father had introduced him to everyone at the Red Owl with a big smile: "But that doesn't mean we don't treat him different. He's just like anybody else, that's all." The boy didn't flinch when they tried not to look too closely at his hearing aid harness.

His father is rather lanky for his height. The boy has never given thought to this before and wonders why some men are so stocky; some, not. Did it have anything to do with their eyes? He tries to remember whether he has seen his father's naked chest before; perhaps, once, he might have, but he is not sure.

The boy decides he's had enough chips. "I'm going over there." The boy points through the flimsy woods; two girls are swinging on the playground. "Bye."

"Be careful," his father says. "Bye-bye."

The boy is swinging quite high when he notices the man again. He is wearing an orange T-shirt with a scratched KEEP ON TRUCKIN' iron-on glittery decal; it's a little tight for his belly. The boy watches him walk back and forth between his picnic table and his rust-chewed Chevy, carrying folding chairs and ice coolers. His wife points out what he should take next as she brushes crumbs off the table and tightens the laces of their two boys' sneakers; her outer thighs jiggle with cellulite as she leans down.

The man tousles both sons' hair and laughs when one of them brushes his hand away. It is a booming laugh, and the boy is surprised by its volume. He wishes everyone's laughter could sound so happy and clear, instead of the nervous type that comes when he can't understand a joke from strangers.

The boy swings harder, until he feels ready to fly from his swing to the branch just above him. As he tenses his feet forward into the dip, he notices the man looking at him strangely: *What are you looking at me for?*

The boy feels embarrassed, for the man had never given any sign he was noticed. He continues swinging with his eyes locked on the man's empty table.

The boy joins his family in the Chevy station wagon, its black seats and trapped air searing inside from the sun. He sits out in the back with his younger brother, while everyone else fits into the two front rows. The boy likes sitting out here, watching the cars fall behind and imagining them racing to keep up with him. Sometimes his younger brother waves and giggles when a surprised driver waves back. Waving is always a wonderful game.

The boy turns around to look at his father, driving and talking quietly as usual, and wonders why he doesn't ever swim.

It is the last Sunday of August, and it is time for the boy to return to Lansel, a university town much larger than where his family lives. He must continue taking speech therapy there; he will stay with a foster family during the week so he can attend school regularly. He's known no other life since his deafness was diagnosed.

"They're here!" His younger brother runs from the front porch to the kitchen where the boy is drinking a glass of Hawaiian Punch. It is almost four-thirty.

His father picks up the suitcase as the driver—an engineering student—turns the key to the trunk of his Impala. They shake hands while his mother hugs the boy and says, "We'll be here on Friday." The rest of his family throws in a discordant chorus of bye-byes and a sprinkle of hands waving as the boy clambers into the back seat and buckles himself in with the familiar seatbelt.

As the driver steers the car out of the driveway, the boy looks back through the window and catches his father's eyes. This time they are sadder and clearer, as if to say, *Why can't you be one of us?* After having kept his head turned, hungry for the fading image of his father, the boy surrenders to the soreness of his neck.

As he settles in for the two and half hours ahead, he wonders about that man's back, dripping brightly with tears above the water.

SALLIE ANN

Funny how time's changed Sallie Ann. Her freckles came out only to tan in the summer, and her smile was real white, except one of her teeth was crooked. Her family hadn't been able to afford a dentist. If they had, her smile would've killed all of my customers. She worked every day from Wednesday to Sunday, with the next two days off. If she called in sick, I knew she'd curled up with one of those cheap romances she found in K-Mart or slept all day while the TV blasted away. She always had to have everything loud.

I met her when she was thirteen. I told her Ma she could wash the dishes in my diner's kitchen, but she turned out to be a better cook than dishwasher. So I gave her better pay and she stayed on for a couple years.

Her strawberry shortcake was the best—she always had to make at least three of 'em on Wednesdays 'cause all the truckers would stop by and wait for 'em to come right out of the oven. And she knew how each trucker liked his eggs and ham. She had one hell of a memory. It was not long before they came by in the evenings too, just for her cooking. Their wives must've cringed when their trucker husbands returned from the road and sang Sallie Ann's praises.

Sometimes when I looked at her, I started thinkin' about my wife Eva and my boy, the way things were before they died in the fire. Since then I've been living above my diner. If you drive by real slow, you can catch me standing in the window behind the orange neon sign that says DAN'S BIG PLACE. It's four miles west of Sandusky, near the Cedar Point Amusement Park.

Sallie Ann and I never had one of them heart-to-heart talks, 'cause I was the cashier and manager and janitor and whatnot. I wanted real bad to have that talk, but time never gave us the chance.

Well, she never gave me the chance.

She had this silly laugh that came straight up from her guts. I loved her laugh. Everybody must've or they wouldn't have told her so many elephant jokes. Oh, she was nuts about those.

She got along with just about everybody, but I knew when she was all alone in the kitchen, she wasn't real happy. She looked thoughtful, but it wasn't a good thoughtful. She came from a big family, but nobody from her family stood out in my mind except that deaf boy. Eddie looked sadder than Sallie Ann, but whenever he came in and saw her, he lit up. They always seemed to understand each other better than anybody. She'd bend down and speak direct to him.

Sallie Ann had been working for me for a while when her whole family stopped by for a meal one Sunday. I tell you, she had one hell of a time trying to introduce all her brothers and sisters to the customers. I could tell she wanted to explain about her deaf brother, but her dad just didn't want anyone to know that he was different.

Anyway, when they left, Sallie Ann was crying over the stove, and away from everybody.

I asked, "What's wrong?"

"They don't want Eddie."

"Who's 'they'?"

"Mom and Dad."

"Why?"

"They expect God to answer their prayers and when He doesn't, I have to take care of things." Then she straightened her shoulders and asked, "What's the next order?"

Some time later she met this guy Lee, and they got married after six months. They went downstate to Dayton. Then I heard they divorced and Lee left for Japan. He was in the Navy or something.

I never saw that deaf guy Eddie again until he came in one day. He had a scrawny moustache and walked less funny than before; he was tall as a cornstalk. He came in with this big guy who looked like a trucker with a fat ass.

"Hey, there!" I asked Eddie direct, "How's Sallie Ann?"

He said, "She doing real good." I was real surprised that he could talk because I didn't recall him speaking at all. I always thought he'd use sign language or something; there's a deaf school downstate in Columbus.

"What's she doin' now?"

"She's still in Dayton."

"How's your parents doin'?"

"Fine. Fine."

"What've you been doin' these days?"

"I live in Columbus."

"The big city, eh? What do you do for a livin'?"

"Computers."

His trucker friend kept looking at me with a big question mark.

I gave him a look. "Sallie Ann used to work for me, okay?"

"Oh," he said. "I'm her husband."

Eddie said, "Sallie Ann married again. This is Jim. And this is Dan."

Jim nodded. He was in no mood to shoot the breeze some.

"Well, what would you guys like?"

He said, "Coffee with cream," and Eddie said, "The same."

An hour later they left a nice tip.

Last week the truckers yelled, "Looky here, it's Sallie Ann! How you been?"

I came running out of the kitchen and there she was, giggling like yesterday. She gained some weight but she looked real nice with that wavy perm. Her dimples never changed, thank God.

She wriggled her fingers and then we hugged. "Dan, you're still here."

"I can't believe it myself, either."

"Oh God," she said. "It's been too long."

"Want some coffee?"

"Nah." She shook her head. "Too much caffeine."

"Time catchin' up on you, eh?"

She nodded. "How you doing these days?"

"Pretty good. You know, they still ask for you. They miss you."

She giggled. "They do? God, we oughta throw a party here."

I smiled. That's what I really missed—she'd help anybody if she heard about a trucker havin' problems with his wife or something. "How about Wednesday night?"

"Seven o'clock?"

"Great. I'll get the word out."

Out the door she went.

One of the truckers caught the look in my eye. "Hey, nothin' like her. Nothin'."

I went back to the kitchen and finished the dishes. It had been a real long time since I thought about Eva.

That Wednesday everybody showed up. I never thought so many would remember for so long; word had gotten around. They even brought along some presents and I made a cake. Then seven o'clock came, but no Sallie Ann. Vern said, "Nothin' new, my wife's always late for church."

We all guffawed.

Fifteen minutes later Sallie Ann showed up. Everybody clapped and gave her kisses on the cheek. Some even pinched her ass, but she brushed 'em all off with a giggle. She said, "Remember you're looking at a married lady."

They said, "Hey, you used to look at us marrieds."

Then one of the truckers gave her a book of elephant jokes and before we knew it, we were all laughing so hard with her. It was so great.

When they all left, it was three in the morning. She insisted on staying to help me clean up the mess.

I was sweeping the paper plates off the counter into the trashcan when I heard her crying in the kitchen. "Sallie Ann, what's wrong?"

She looked at me. "You know what I really miss? Working here."

"Well, I don't make money like I used to. They got all those fast food chains down the highway right up to Cedar Point, you know."

"Oh, it's all right. I had the best times here. I just never knew how much I missed this place."

I wanted so much to offer her my apartment, my place, my everything, but she was married.

"You remember Eddie? My deaf brother? He doesn't talk to my family anymore." She made a real deep sigh and said, "Why is it that once you say goodbye, it's never the same?"

"Dunno. Life, maybe?"

She looked down and said nothing.

When I finished sweeping, she moved to the front counter like a ravenous trucker at three-thirty in the morning. I decided to tease her a bit. "Been on the road, eh? What'd you like?"

"Nothing," she said. "I'm not hungry."

"Hey. It's on me."

"Been a while since I felt needed, you know?" She shrugged. "Well. Gotta go or Jim's gonna think I'm screwing some stupid-ass trucker."

I laughed. She wriggled her fingers and before I knew it, she was gone.

I never saw her again. Guess it's better that way.

ESPIONAGE

I am reading in my room when I hear glass break. I want to get up and tell my Deaf parents to stop fighting, but the fact is, they've been doing this all my life. I adjust my underwear and fall back on my bed. I turn down the volume of my stereo a little. I'm playing some U2.

Finally I hear a dull thud, as if a heavy book was flung at the wall. I get up and go down the stairs, knowing they will censor their dirty language if they see me. They haven't yet; I stand in the doorway to the living room.

Dad's been drinking a long time now. Sometimes I wonder if it's because he can't stand the fact that I'm hearing. I always end up interpreting for him, and then he doesn't trust anything I repeat. But I know my Mom has a lot of faith in me. When I was fourteen and ashamed of my parents, Grandma told me that when I was born, Mom wouldn't sign in front of me until one day she saw that I never cried for my bottle on the mantel. I simply pointed to it.

Mom tries so hard to make Dad happy, but he won't take her as she is although everybody likes her and says things like, "Oh, sign language is so beautiful," or "You're so deaf, it's amazing that your boy can talk at all." I have long since learned not to raise my voice in anger; it doesn't change anything.

I watch Dad standing near the fat lime couch with a broken tumbler at Mom's feet. He's shutting her out as usual. This is his last word: No one tells him what to do because he pays the mortgage. He has been at the post office for twenty-seven years; Mom has been working all along with preschool kids at the Deaf school on Burton Avenue.

Dad heads for the kitchen where his bottles, placed on the top shelf in the taller cabinet, await his thirsty reach.

Mom turns and looks for me in the doorway. She knows I'm always close by to protect her. I have no other reason for staying here, even though it'd be easier to live closer to downtown where I work.

Her eyes are sad. When she's like that, I always want to say something, but I repeat instead in ASL, "You brave woman you-can."

I told her that a few months ago. She took me aside and asked me about the idea of divorce. This was so like her: She always asks me how I feel about any important decision she must make. I told her, like I tell all my friends, it was her own decision, and no one else's to make. She sat on my bed and asked me over and over again, and I sighed. Dad is as demanding too, but he never believes me.

"We-two discuss now." When she says this, I know she wants to go up to my room where she knows Dad will never walk in on us. She sits beside me on my bed. Dad never wanted to marry her in the first place, but she was pregnant with me. She doesn't want to leave this house. She's invested too much of herself in the hope of making Dad smile again. "Ideas any?"

I say nothing; I don't want to give her any.

She stands up.

I look into her eyes and I know what she's decided.

"Interpret lawyer can?"

I turn toward my stereo. Adam Clayton and Larry Mullen Jr.'s remake of "Theme from *Mission Impossible*" is playing.

She flaps her hand within my peripheral vision. "Please."

"Why me? Not-want involve." I want to turn up the music. Sometimes I feel like puncturing my own eardrums. I get up toward the music, but I change my mind. I take my suitcase out of my closet. "You-need?"

"Where sleep where?"

I say nothing as she lifts the suitcase and inspects its wheels.

"Edna?" she asks. Edna is her best friend.

Mom stares at me. I've forgotten about Edna's husband seeing a hearing woman. "Can't two-you roommates can't?"

"N-o." This is so like her; she wants help from no one, yet expects mine. She leaves my room, dragging my suitcase down the hallway to her bedroom. I can hear her shuttling between the hangers, her packing of clothes, and her slamming the drawers. When I hear Dad turn on the TV, I turn up my stereo. I want my speakers to transmit vibrations down to Dad and collide with the closed captions beneath Anderson Cooper.

I try reading my book, but it's just impossible. My mind's

elsewhere with all those conflicting sounds. I put my book down and close my eyes. I pretend, as I always have since I first watched an old episode of *The Six-Million-Dollar Man,* that my ears are bionic. I think I hear the brisk twist of Dad's whiskey bottle and the final clamp of my suitcase.

But the music's much too loud, too dense. I turn it down.

This time I can hear the soft moving in her bedroom. I imagine her trying to decide which coat to wear to work tomorrow.

She comes into my room at last. She asks, "Borrow T-T-Y fine?" She is so old-fashioned that she won't get herself a smartphone.

I nod yes.

I'm relieved that she wants to call me with her teletypewriter wherever she goes. I continue moving my head to Larry Mullen Jr.'s machine-gun drumming underneath. I don't want her to know that I'm scared of being alone in this house, or she'll never leave the enemy. He is still a dangerous country, where the passport of language means nothing.

KNOWN | UNKNOWN

She is still a specter who's been hidden deep in my exoskeleton. Sometimes I swear I can feel her breathing right next to my parched skin. She is still alive, and gratefully so. Her presence of memory is a whiplash of ghost and dread. Had I just imagined her waking up next to me only to disappear into the bathroom? I long to see her face, devoid of pretense, again and again. After ten years, I can't get rid of her, nor do I want to. She is something familiar, a well-worn bead in the rosary of my life.

Some hearing people fall in love with certain people because of their voices; sexy in the distinctiveness of such wavelengths pulsing against their eardrums deep inside their souls. Some Deaf people, like myself, fall in love with certain people because of their signing style. She signed almost with a Texan twang, but with a hint of the softness of bluegrass in the backyard of her Kentuckian childhood. She bent with the winds of change much like the way a branch, heavy with apples yet to fall to the ground, rode the coattails of breeze to survive another day without losing its babies. The openness of her eyes bejeweled me as I reduced the big sky above us into the laser beam of what would've been our lives shared together. And all that in a single moment of seeing each other, not even knowing each other's names!

If I had doubted the value of learning Sign, I no longer did in the moment I saw her. I had grown up oral, but I chose to learn Sign in college. She was laughing with a friend at the Deaf Expo; I got the impression that she had just been told a stereotypical joke by her friend. I hadn't seen her before, but she looked great. Beautiful eyes. Sexy chin. Nice wide hips. Despite my best efforts to look disinterested, I hung around long enough to watch her leave her friend behind. I didn't want to seem like a stalker, so I made idle chat with a surprising number of Deaf people who wanted to learn more about becoming poll workers. They had no idea that such opportunities were available to Deaf people; the elections commission had made it a mission to target the Deaf community for volunteers. It was touching to see how some hearing people were so willing to learn and interact with us. I could still speak, but I much preferred to sign. I held more confidence in my fingertips than in my larynx. There was no question in my mind that I would date a Deaf woman. Alas, my ex-wife turned out to be a mistake, but her Deafness had nothing to do with it.

The grass, once green from the lushness of hope lingering in the air between us, turned brown the moment she learned that my ex-wife had been her nemesis at the Deaf residential school where she'd grown up. I had not made the connection between my ex-wife and the woman standing before me until that moment. My ex-wife had blathered on and on about a Jill Lamsky, but I paid her no attention. The past was past, and I was all about the future. The woman who would break my heart had heard horribly untrue stories about me from people who were on Team Jill. I was a bad Jack. The fleeting moment of attraction alighting between our eyes evaporated once I told her my first and last name. She recognized the name instantly, and asked if I was still married. I shook my head no, and I asked her if she was. She shook her head no. Still our eyes lingered on each other as I watched the inner gears working inside her brain, trying to reconcile the nasty stories that my ex-wife and her friends had shared about the man standing tall before her.

That evening we found ourselves naked in my messy bed. It was almost as if we didn't need to talk much between leaving the convention hall and having her car follow mine for three miles back to my place. Once inside, we couldn't taste enough of each other. Moments of fierce ecstasy melted into hours as we rose and ebbed with our tides of desire. We laughed with so much joy emanating from our imperfect bodies. I'd never felt such flashes of authenticity with a woman before. Was it true love? Or just unbridled lust? Whatever it was, it was far superior to anything I'd experienced previously with a woman. Nothing had quite prepared me for the intensity of her. Yet by the time she left past midnight, I somehow knew we would never connect again. She had suddenly remembered the lies her Deaf friends had told her about me; she never asked me whether those stories were true. She never offered me her text number. She had to maintain her standards, her respectability, within the Deaf community. Of course. I may have been just a spark of sex to her, but she was Love Incarnate to me. My bones still ache for her each time I happen to see her around town. I want to tell her that there's such a thing as too much pride.

Flashes of her smile, her body, still blast supernovas into my memory. How I cling on to the fading debris of her as she sails further and further away each night. I never knew how possible it was to love a woman so much I could taste death on my tongue each time I saw her; not wanting to die but being willing to die if it meant her unconditional devotion. I had turned into a mess of nebula, but no one except her had ever known the molten core of my soul.

The minutes spent together have gradually become memories put in perpetual slow motion. I no longer recall the exact signs she'd used when we were together, but the meaning of each sentence has become a drum song that vary unpredictably in tempo whenever I pause to recall. Each moment has become an untitled song, yet it aches for a precise title in order to become properly fossilized in the ambered diorama of my mind. I don't want her to change; I want to preserve her for all time. Different women who pass by me inevitably echo something of her, often offering a most unexpectedly overlooked detail that did not appear in my aches when translated into my slo-mo songs of her. Her name may be Jill Lamsky, but she is much bigger than a single name engraved on the wooden trunk of my heart. Sometimes I have to remind myself that she does have a name. I feel so nameless with her.

Not too long after she'd left my place, she changed, trading warmth for a mask of ice. I had become a blemish best forgotten. I look at myself in the mirror every day and ask just what it was about me that had turned her off so. Had I said something wrong? Had I not satisfied her enough? Hadn't she begged for a third round? To this day, she has never said a word to me. I don't like the fact that I've gotten too good at waiting for clarification. Sometimes I make a point of warming my own hands in case she wants me to stand before her, and feel that my hands are warm enough to melt away her icy reserve. She would bloom and make me forget the sadness that has long replicated inside my bones.

Other Deaf women may come and go in my life, but I've become less and less interested as the years roll on by. They will never compare to her. We will all grow old one day, but she will always be as young as the day I met her. If she cares to look, she will find me waiting right here at each Deaf event around town. When her friends finally abandon her for the silliest of reasons, I'll be right here like the North Star, never wavering from my place in the twilit sky. I am always watching out for her. All she needs to do is smile at me like the first time she caught me without knowing who I was. I want to be unknown again and start over.

MAFIA BUTTERFLY

No one who knows me will ever tell you this, but I'm a butterfly.

I'm not even talking about the clichéd hearing view of my hands signing as if they are pretty monarchs fluttering around, or the fact that I'm a full-grown Deaf woman, who's full capital-D. People would say that at twenty-seven years old, I'm in the prime of my life. Guys especially notice me when I walk down the street. I am never sure if it's because of the way my hair flips about in the wind or that I'm wearing clothes that fit me well. I never turn my head to look back. It's really nice to keep my hearing aids turned off when I'm outside. This way I don't overhear the catcalls.

No one makes a move to ask me out once they see I can't speak very well.

Let me retract that. They've certainly tried, but they keep looking down at my body. Uh-*uh*. I'm much more than the sum of my body parts. Oh, so much more. I'm always astonished at how men are willing to reduce themselves to the only body part that matters to them.

The minute I open my mouth to speak, everything changes in a second.

Suddenly they're not in power.

I make it crystal clear that I don't need them to complete me.

That drives them nuts. Good!

They need to get over themselves.

It's the language, baby. If they don't know how to sign, I'm not interested.

It's clear on their faces that they assume if I'm Deaf, I must be all about the body, as if my lack of speech has reduced me to the level of an animal ready to writhe about in the mud. I am tired of the joke that Deaf people are supposed to be great in bed because they don't know how to say no. Ha ha, right. They got that wrong. I am great in bed because I know *how* to say yes, and only when I'm ready.

Some people think I'm a woman of mystery. Having grown up in a hearing family has made it possible for me to keep myself cloaked on a need-to-know basis. I still keep in touch with my two sisters, but only through email. They always look lost when we meet in person. They can't sign. They apologize again for not having the time to learn, but that's precisely when they know to stop talking about it. They know I'll remind them that I took fourteen years of speech therapy for their benefit. What could be so hard about taking classes? It's all about priorities, people.

Deaf people around here know who I am, but I don't hang out at Deaf events like I used to. I keep track of them on Facebook, but that's it.

I'm not going to name names here, but there's a Deaf man who still gives me dirty looks. He's in his sixties. Married with three kids and seven grandchildren. He talks about them all the time. People say he's very nice, and he's popular. But he's like the mafia boss of the Deaf community around here.

I'm not talking about the mafia that you see in the *Godfather* movies.

Little Italy's been long gone, you know.

The mafia doesn't need guns to exercise its power. The threat of excommunication is sufficient. It's a certain look that comes from having been in the community long enough to be considered worthy of respect, and who has been endowed the unassailable power of persuasion.

I'm talking about how Deaf people look to the mafia boss for guidance on whether to accept a new Deaf member or not. They always invite him to their parties and into their homes for dinner. They always hug and take forever with their long goodbyes.

When I show up at a sign-interpreted theater performance, they say hello and move on.

I try not to take it personally, but I do.

What have I done to merit dismissal?

I've never attacked anyone. Never!

I have a full-time job that I love. I design book covers and marketing materials for the biggest publisher in town. Visual language was mine long before I was allowed to learn Sign as a teenager.

When I tasted the forbidden fruit of Sign, I suddenly realized that I had been sleeping all my life in a cocoon.

I grasped the power of letting my hands out in the open.

I was announcing to the world that I was different. I didn't have to pretend to be hearing, or a hard of hearing person.

I wasn't just deaf; I was Deaf. Capital-D!

Yay, right?

I made my way to my first Deaf social gathering at a coffeehouse. At first I felt scared. I thought they'd accept me because I'd taken the time to learn Sign from videos online and read up on Deaf history. No one said hello to me when I sat two tables over. I didn't want to seem pushy. After all, I was a frightened teenager with pimples on my face.

Watching them carry on as if no one else existed, I wanted to die from my own stupidity.

I had hoped to say, "I know sign language, too," but watching them made me feel so small. There was no way I could possibly be as fluent as they were.

After I finished my bottle of soda, I slunk out of there.

To this day I am amazed and yet angered that no one ever noticed the wide-eyed fear on my face. Did they think they didn't need another Deaf person in the community?

Apparently not.

I cried every night until I felt nothing but stone in my heart.

When I graduated from high school, I decided not to go to Gallaudet University or the National Technical Institute for the Deaf. The coldness of these people at the coffeehouse broke me into a thousand and one pieces. I went to Browell University right here. My parents aren't made of money, and neither was I.

I took ASL classes at Browell. Foreign language requirement, you know?

My teacher Peggy Whitehead was the best. She was so excited to have a Deaf student in her class for a change. She saw how quickly I mastered the vocabulary. The idioms and syntax were a bit difficult at first, but I discovered that as long as I didn't think about how I was signing, everything in Sign made perfect sense. Thinking in English was the problem.

I felt closer to home, but it kept drifting away each time I showed up at a Deaf event. Peggy and I became good friends after I graduated from college, and she introduced me to so many people.

I didn't know at first that the Deaf mafia boss had a thing against her when I met him. I didn't know how she had stood up to him years before. The fact that she'd grown up in a Deaf family made it impossible for him to dismiss her so easily. He mocked her behind her back, and she had learned about this from their mutual friends.

Before she finally introduced me to him after an ASL-interpreted show, she warned me about him. "Himself same-same m-a-f-i-a decide maybe you nothing. If happens, worry not. Himself run Deaf community not. Courtesy-show respect nice, that-all."

I recognized him from the first time I attended a Deaf social gathering. He was a bit older than I'd recalled. He had a nice smile. I liked him immediately. I wished he were my father.

Peggy beckoned me to come closer. "Want introduce you him." She told him my name, and we shook hands.

"Nice meet-you." I smiled.

"Herself learn Sign fast. My first Deaf ASL student. Proud her!" She squeezed my arm and hugged me.

A warm glow rose in me. I wished she were my real mother. "Thank-you," I said.

He gave me a look that said, *Oh, I see*. The slight distaste was clear in his eyes. "Go home now must. Sorry." He turned to Peggy. "Take-care."

She gave him a stony smile at his backside. "Bastard," she said once he left the lobby and turned to me. "Warn you finish."

I nodded.

"Other friends find can."

So I did.

Each time I showed up to Deaf events with friends who signed, he and his friends looked away from me. Some of my friends were hearing ASL students; a few of them used to be my interpreters in college. I didn't believe in discriminating against friends who were hearing.

I began to notice something else about him.

You do know who I'm talking about, right?

Yep, that's him.

So you know how he walks around, like he's something of a politician, when he mingles among his friends. Sometimes a friend of his would introduce him to someone new. If the new person was truly fluent in ASL or had come from a Deaf family, he would banter with his jokes.

If she wasn't, tough luck.

Peggy is right. Why are we supposed to kiss the ring finger of the mafia? If we don't, is that so bad? Why are many Deaf people so afraid about being judged when they choose to befriend a new Deaf person? Can't they see that it isn't healthy to dismiss people they barely know? We need more Deaf friends.

I want to be accepted as I am. I used to be a lousy signer, but Peggy says that I'm very fluent in ASL now. She says I'm the best student she's ever had.

She's taught me so much.

She showed me how important it was to stay strong no matter what.

Strength isn't always contained in my hands. Strength comes from choosing how to use my hands in the most effective way possible.

I choose to mingle among my own friends. I do not worry about the Deaf mafia don or the fact that his cronies have made a point of ignoring me or Peggy. They will eventually die.

It can be so hard, though, being a butterfly when no one tenders you a flower for you to perch on for a moment of respite. Isn't that what community is supposed to be about?

No matter what anyone says, I am a butterfly. I will continue to live my life as honestly as I can, and flit about, practicing my future powers of persuasion, so that one day I will live long enough and be made mafia boss myself, and accept everyone, no matter how badly they may sign.

It isn't just the language that matters. What's in your heart does, too.

POSTER CHILD ’95

[*in ASL gloss*]

Picture girl look good. T-T-Y number there, good idea. Maybe Deaf see her too.

What? Interpreter sit-there perfect. Me-ready now.

Me-accused kidnapping? What-for-for?

Nosy-nosy food me-buy what, can’t believe privacy none.

All-right, all-right. Me-tell-you explain again two-days-ago. Me-work principal office same-same when someone-walk-up-to-me girl short-cute-cute, age six, maybe eight. Saw her around before, but name blank-mind that time. No one in office, just-the-two-of-us. R-e-c-e-s-s time, you-know?

Ask-her, “Help need?”

Ask-me, “Need kid you-need?”

“Have kids finish. Why?”

“Mom-Dad don’t-want.”

Mind-blocked. Girl herself young. “Unh—why?”

“Me-sit home watch open-lips-like-clown-stupid at me, me wish in school already.”

“Sorry. Maybe parents learn signs will.”

“They-don’t-care.”

“Dorm supervisor who?”

“Doris-Davies.”

“Discuss two-of-us will, figure-out do-do. Go play.”

Her-gone, mind-blocked still. Couldn’t focus work. Give-up, search Doris-Davies, not there, came back office, continue working. Mind-obsessed girl still, but continued working. Found Doris-Davies dorm; found her upset. Girl disappeared-from-surface. Everyone looked-looked. That all information me-have girl.

Me-take her? Silly you. Of-course not. Afford take-care kids can’t.

W-h-a-t?

Me-take her not. Understand?

My house? No way. Go-there can't. My house, not yours.

That poster up-there smart. Pretty. Awful, awful gone. Wish quick adopt could. Then safe for sure. You-know?

LISTENING

The weight of blood in my son Reese has cast a dusty shadow in every step he leaves behind. I want to be clear as water, but I am all blood. I have hurt him much too much. I am the face of disrespect. He has no interest in hearing my voice again.

It's the day after his high school graduation, and he is already in surgery.

When Reese was born, I thought he was the most beautiful thing ever. He evoked angels when he slept in my arms. My entire being swelled with so much hope. This time a child would have the best father in the world, unlike my own who hadn't treated us kids well. Our father rarely talked much while I was growing up. His presence was an emotional black hole at the table. We kids never knew how to make conversation with him. If we talked with each other while eating, we talked quietly. We were always careful not to clink our forks and spoons against our plates and bowls. The dining room was almost a cathedral where every meal was a Mass. But there was never a hymnal. Those meals with our father never had much joy.

Years later I would ask out loud what our mother had seen in him. We saw pictures of her from when she was younger. Her hair was a spitfire of henna. She was always smiling or laughing. But when she began having us kids, one after another, she gained weight. She became monolithic, a statue that demanded a pious worship. Her face was a pool of tears ready to waterfall.

None of us kids knew the answer to my question.

Until we began marrying, we didn't understand how marriage can change people.

We also didn't understand how children could change people until we began having them.

Growing up in the woods, set far in the backyard behind the barn,

I felt weightless. I could feel the blades of sunlight saw through me easily. My bones felt warmed with joy. I didn't need to think about the darkness that persisted in the house even with the shades pulled up.

Out among the trees, everything was all air. No walls anywhere. The sun always flitted like a train of laughter around me. Bird calls reverberated everywhere.

After too many broken seasons where not enough crops grew on the land, our parents made the unexpected decision to sell the farm and we relocated to a small house on the edge of town. We were vastly disappointed when we saw how the smallness of their new house had failed to expel the same darkness from the old farmhouse.

By then each of us had trickled out into the great wide world. I was the youngest one, the one left behind, wondering what my own adventures after high school would be like.

Walking past the houses in our neighborhood, I wondered if each one of them was also packed with darkness. Did the neighbors speak only in the language of silence when alone with each other?

And what about their children?

I intuitively sensed that those questions, if asked out loud, were a dangerous minefield. The fabric of society itself would surely collapse.

When Reese turned one year old, I sensed that something was off. My wife insisted that everything was fine. *Look at him, running already*. We had to laugh every time he made a point of sneaking off to run somewhere. Our golden retriever Margee made a point of always getting up from the floor to follow him when Reese disappeared. We soon learned that meant Reese was venturing into dangerous territory again.

Then he came down with meningitis. Our darkest fear was confirmed: He had gone deaf.

Until then I had felt utter joy with my wife Kelly. She was the first bite of an orange, a jonquil burst of color, a ripple of laughter echoing off a burbling creek. I felt as if all the dark passages in my soul were lit by the radiance of her smiles. I couldn't get enough of holding her hand in public. She was *mine.*

She was shocked when she met my parents for the first time. "They're only in their fifties, but they're so *old*. I can't quite explain it."

I nodded.

The darkness that I didn't want from my parents' house found its way into the space between my son and me. I wanted to embrace him and fill him with the brilliant light of sound and speech and understanding, but something in his eyes had shifted. A new weight had taken hold of him in the pit of his soul. He would have to navigate the world more carefully now that he had the cochlear implants in his head. It crushed my heart that he wouldn't be able to play football like I had. If he had to undergo an MRI, he'd need to have surgery to remove the implants first. In the future he'd need to show proof of his implants each time he bypassed the security screening before he got on a plane. I looked at the round magnets docked on the back of his head and felt a twinge of uneasiness. Yes, I knew the implants were to help him hear, but the magnets broadcast to the world that he was different: *Look behind my head and you'll see a freak.*

In time I became accustomed to seeing his magnets much like glasses that people wore on their noses, but I could never get used to seeing the reactions of strangers on the street when they saw them. They inevitably said, "But isn't he *too* young to have them?"

I learned not to show indignancy. How dare they share their opinions with me, a stranger, as if they knew better than I what it was like to have a deaf child?

Kelly and I took Reese and Margee for walks through the woods where we would be sure not to run into strangers who'd insist on stopping us to gawk at our baby in the stroller. We did not need human eyes judging us.

It never occurred to us that our son would eventually judge us.

The darkness soon spread into the space between my wife and me. She was terrified of having another baby only to have it go deaf again. I tried to reason with her that meningitis was actually a rare occurrence, but it was to no avail. She went on the pill, and things weren't the same after that. Our sex turned dull. Our orgasms, if any, no longer exploded sunlight. Sex once a month had become a duty like washing dishes and taking out the garbage.

She still held Reese close to her bosom, but it wasn't the same. He'd intuited that something was not quite right with him, but he'd already forgotten what it was like to hear normally.

Each day at the office I thought about the darkness expanding among the three of us. I was proud of the progress that Reese was making with his speech therapy. It was something of an adjustment, though, to keep remembering that we had to keep our faces trained on his while speaking with him.

Worse was the fact that when it was time to replace and upgrade the implants after ten years, which was an extraordinarily long time for an implant to last, Reese insisted on not going to the hospital. The pamphlet that was designed to explain the surgery in simple terms to deaf children had terrified him. He shook his head *no no no*. He was turning twelve.

More unsettling was the fact that he typically used his voice; but this time he did so with a new silence suddenly his.

Kelly tried to plead with him to reconsider. But he was obstinate.

I had never seen such stubbornness in him before. I wondered where it was coming from. None of his deaf classmates had issues with having their implants upgraded.

By this point I had read several Deaf memoirs, hoping to eradicate the darkness in our home. The authors all said that when they were alone with other deaf oralists, they always used their hands. It was their innate birthright, they said. That was my main takeaway from the books.

The darkness that shadowed our son was full of octopus hands. Sign language would take him away from me. Politics, too. I shook my head no, but I had to be pragmatic. Anything was indeed possible with our son.

But Kelly insisted that he would not succeed as well if he signed instead of speaking. He was doing really well in school.

I sat Reese down on the living room sofa and looked carefully at him. I knew there was enough light on my face. It was the night before his scheduled surgery.

"Reese," I said while I gestured to my ears in spite of myself. "I know you don't want the new implants, but it's really important that you get to hear better."

He shook his head no.

"Please. Your mom and I want you to hear better and be happy."

"I'm tired of headaches."

I nodded. He had complained about them for a long time. The pain meds hadn't seemed to be of much help. "I think the new ones will make the headaches go away."

He gave me a look that said everything all at once: *Yeah right. Are you trying to lie to me so you can make Mom happy even if it could mean more headaches for me?*

Never before had two words—*I'm sorry*—seemed so inadequate.

Later that night Kelly whispered, "I hate you. You couldn't even convince him!"

I could not sleep all that night. The darkness between us that was once a river had widened into an ocean. To cross to the other side meant drowning.

Our bed became a raft with no compass. Only Reese had buoyed us together in the ocean.

On the gurney, he kicked and screamed so loudly that the anesthesiologist had to tranquilize him.

It was frightening to watch how a single injection could transform a flailing person.

I was the last face he saw before he fell limp.

The anger in his eyes was still molten lava.

When Reese underwent his first implant surgery, Kelly and I held hands the entire time in the waiting room. We were too tense to talk. The pulsing between our palms back and forth did all the talking.

She wept when we saw how the surgeon had wrapped Reese's head. He was still asleep.

When he finally awakened, he looked woozily at us. I saw flickers of pain and fear in his eyes. What had just happened to him?

I held him close to my chest and exhaled slowly.

He needed to know that I too felt his pain. If I could have the surgery done on me so that he didn't have to undergo that pain alone,

I'd have done it. I prayed that he'd sense my sentiments in the cradle of my arms.

This time, though, for his second surgery, Kelly and I didn't hold hands.

Much to our relief, Reese didn't lash out at us in the days after he woke up from the second procedure. He didn't say much.

It was the first time that I began to see he was no longer a boy even though he was not yet a teenager. He had the eyes of an old man. Such resentment, such brittleness.

In the aloneness of my car on my way to the office, I wept.

Kelly never knew.

By the time Reese turned thirteen, Kelly and I had divorced. We never argued. We simply agreed to share custody.

Our child had become a business transaction, a formality that required our signatures on the bottom line.

Only a few awkward words were spoken between us when we sat with our attorney.

The official term is "irreconcilable differences," but we had no language left to describe the darkness that had marooned us.

Our go-to explanation was the simplest: "It just didn't work out."

Each time Reese stayed with me every other week, I tried to get him to go outside with me. I had a new collie named Martha. She never left his side when he showed up. He always laughed when she nuzzled her nose into his armpits. I loved the sound of his laughter. *So pure.*

It was so hard to make conversation when he didn't want to speak. I thought perhaps it was because he had become a morose teenager.

Yet, according to his teachers, he was doing very well in classes. If I may say so, his speech was quite exceptional compared to his other deaf peers even though they had implants too. I was relieved that he didn't try to sign.

I didn't want to be like my father. I wanted to be a ray of sunlight, a jolt of joy that would make everyone feel welcome.

On the very next day after his high school graduation, he planted himself happily on the gurney. "Bring it on," he said. I had never seen him so full of light, bursting with hope. He no longer wanted the implants in his head. He had finally become old enough to decide his own future.

The implants had reminded him of the pain of us hearing people. He wanted to move away to college where he could learn ASL and be with other Deaf people because they had nothing to do with his hearing parents.

We had become a dull headache.

That hurt.

It would be decades before Kelly and I realized that we had asked the wrong questions.

We had no words left to express our shock when we saw the first of his post-surgery pictures on social media. He was happy! He even bragged about never wanting to hear again. After all, he didn't have any more headaches. He shared videos of himself learning new ASL signs. Then came his hurtful stories about how lonely he had been at school while growing up; apparently his teachers hadn't wanted to delve too deeply into whether their deaf students were happy socially. He eventually became a teacher and an activist for bilingual access in Deaf education.

Then came the unexpected news. He had married and become a father to a Deaf baby girl. She was already signing right back!

I didn't know whether to be proud or weep.

During his implant removal surgery, Kelly and I sat in the waiting room.

"I think we've failed him," I said quietly. "We just didn't want to listen."

She looked up at me and held my hand for the first time in forever.

RASPBERRIES

I like picking raspberries because they taste good. It's a fun thing to do on a summer day. Today Mom and Dad are shopping for food. Then they will bring Grandma home from the hospital. She had a car accident so she can't walk anymore. I visited her every day, but today's special because she's coming home.

Picking raspberries makes my fingers go red, and then I have to lick them all over, like my dog Fuzzy. But he don't like to get near the raspberries in Grandpa's yard because of the thorns. He just sits in the shade, panting from the heat and watching me from the other side of the fence. He's got pale blue eyes with a black and white shaggy coat; he's supposed to be half border collie, but no one knows what the other half is. I can't always understand people on the street when we go walking, but I can see their faces when they see Fuzzy wagging his big tail, and then they see my hearing aids. All of a sudden their faces sink and they go quiet. It's so strange because my family don't act scared of me or look like they're sad for me. Sometimes people on the street talk real loud or show off their teeth when they think I can't lipread them at all. They seem to think I need a lot of help, but I don't. My neighbors are good about waving to me and petting Fuzzy while they ask me how I'm doing.

Anyway, Fuzzy always follows me without a leash wherever I go, even on the street. But not when I pick raspberries. After I fill my plastic bucket to the brim, I look for one last raspberry hidden under all the leaves and pop it into my mouth. I allow myself to eat only one raspberry when I pick them. My brothers are terrible at raspberries. They never pick enough to make a rhubarb-raspberry pie, they keep picking and eating them as they go along. Grandma says I'm the best picker. Maybe it's because I'm a girl.

Out here is Grandpa's place. There's a big garden that he weeds all the time, and it's got a big lawn that he mows twice a week. He's got a big garage and a dull green truck that's real old. He said his father used it during the Great Depression, which sounds like a long time ago, so he likes to keep it working. It's a fat truck, but he's proud of it. I went riding in the open back with my brothers to the beach one time. It was loud and it bumped a lot on the street. It was fun to sit and feel the air. I had to keep Fuzzy on the leash that one time. Dad was afraid Fuzzy would jump out of the truck on the highway, but he didn't. He stuck his head out and let the wind whip at his nose. He drooled all over my brothers so they moved to the other side of the truck. I just held on to him. I didn't want him to jump out.

Anyway, my bucket is nice and heavy. It's got just enough for the pie that Grandma says she'll make when she comes home. I close the gate behind me, and Fuzzy is already sniffing at my hands. I set the bucket down on the grass and let him lick my hands with his long tongue. His pink tongue turns red, and then his nose is about to dive into the bucket. I scream "No!" He scurries away a little back to the garden fence where there's chicken wire and wooden posts. Grandpa made the fence very tall to keep the deer out. He did the same thing for the raspberries. I have to keep the gate closed at all times. Grandpa dug deep around the fence and installed mosquito screens so the rabbits wouldn't have an easy time getting into the patch. He did the same thing for the garden. That was a big job, but all of us helped out. I pushed the dirt back into the trench when the screens were put in. My brothers and I had a lot of fun stamping on the dirt, packing it down.

Over by the garden Fuzzy spins around and trots right back to me. He looks into my eyes, and he drops suddenly to the ground and sticks his butt up. He wants to play. So I put my bucket onto the back of Grandpa's truck and go rolling around in the grass with him. He loves wrestling with me, and he never bites me. Never. That's what a good dog he is.

We go on chasing each other. He darts away when I think I got him in my arms, and then he lies on his back. He wants a belly rub. He reaches up to lick my face if I lean too close. He always makes me laugh when he does that. I don't know what time it is yet, but I have to get ready for Grandma. I think she will like the new ramp that Dad and Uncle Steve built for her. It took them two days to build. Fuzzy likes to chase the ball down the ramp when it bounces away to the sidewalk, and he brings it back to me. But Dad says I can't do that anymore. The ramp is for Grandma only. You don't have to climb steps to the front door like before. I helped Dad paint the wood green and white to match the house. I had to tie Fuzzy to the mailbox post so he wouldn't get too close to the wet paint. Grandpa didn't help out. He was too busy fixing something in the garage. Dad and Uncle Steve kept looking at each other like there was something wrong with Grandpa. They didn't talk much so I didn't know why. They told me not to go into the garage.

The house has a nice lemony smell. We call it Grandma's house because she's the one who keeps it clean. She washes the floors once a week so it's always shiny. I like the hardwood floors in the dining room the best. The sun glows there in the afternoon. I like the way it dances through the curtains when the breeze blows in. Sometimes the floors are like a mirror, and you have to hide your eyes a bit. We don't have hardwood floors in my house, so it's different. Everything feels so ready for Grandma's return, but I know she will be upset to see that the cabinets in the dining room haven't been dusted in a while. Mom tried her best, but she was so busy taking care of Grandma at the hospital. I tried to help out, but Mom didn't want me to climb up the ladder. My brothers didn't want to dust. They said it was too girlie.

I carry my bucket to the side door of Grandma's house. There's no ramp, but you can go downstairs or upstairs to the kitchen, so I hold the door to let Fuzzy in before me. He goes straight upstairs to his bowl of water by the shoe mat and starts drinking greedily, and then he lies right near the air conditioner in the dining room while I show Grandpa my bucket. He is sitting at the kitchen table, reading a newspaper. He's got a big belly, and he's got a red scar across his forehead. He got it from a war in Vietnam. I always mispronounce that name. I say it as "Veet-nam," but everyone tells me it's "Vee-it-nam." The "it" syllable is very small. I practice words a lot. He has a thick white moustache, but he keeps it very short so I can see his lips.

He says, "Let me see your tongue."

I stick it out to show that I've had only one raspberry.

He nods approval.

"Check Fuzzy too."

Fuzzy wakes up when he hears his name. He's real funny when one of his ears go up like that.

"Fuzzy, Fuzzy. Come here."

He comes up to me and lets me open his jaw. Grandpa looks down and smiles. "A little guilty, but acceptable." He chuckles.

I hide the bucket in a big plastic bag and tuck it in the back of the fridge where my brothers won't find it so easy. They're out in Logan Park, playing baseball. I don't like being around when they play baseball because they always act like big shots. They're all older than me. They say girls don't know how to play ball. Not true. Sometimes they pretend they don't know me, 'specially when other kids point at my ears. I never know exactly what my brothers say to them. They hate it when I ask. I hate it even more when they don't answer.

Fuzzy was supposed to belong to Keith, my oldest brother, but he didn't like Keith at all. He took one sniff of me, and that was it. He's stayed with me ever since he was a puppy. He didn't want to play with my brothers. Maybe that's why Keith don't like me so much. He's in ninth grade now. Dad says that Keith's going through changes most people don't understand, but I will understand when my turn comes. I hate it when grownups talk like that. Maybe Dad thinks because I can't hear everything, I won't be able to understand everything. Not true.

My other two brothers just follow Keith around. Sometimes I want to follow, but not all the time because they push me around and say that I can't do certain things because I'm a girl. They hate it when I keep asking what things, what stuff. That's why they always slip out and never tell me where they're going. They think I'm such a big mouth. But they do talk a lot, and I can't always understand their jokes. Sometimes I think they're stupid, but Mom says that I shouldn't think those things about them. It's not nice. I'm supposed to give them a chance to talk, and then they'll give me a chance to talk. I don't know why people have to talk all at the same time. Mom says it's rude too. That's why I like Fuzzy. He don't tell me that I can't do anything, and he don't tell anyone what things I've done. Grandpa goes back to the living room and watches TV. I sit on the sofa, and Fuzzy follows. He knows he can't jump up on the sofa so he rests his head on the edge of the sofa and waits for me to pet him. On TV, some soldiers are shooting a small group of thin people. They are almost like skeletons when they collapse to the ground. Other soldiers stand and watch them die, not even moving to help. I can't see their faces well because it was done on a video camera like Dad's. Grandpa turns and catches me watching. He picks up his remote control and changes the channel. A nature program comes on, and it's got captions.

Fuzzy and I watch the whole thing. It's all about butterflies and moths. I watch some men go netting after the butterflies, which I find very strange. Why chase the butterflies when they will let you watch them a few feet away if you stay still? That's how I watch butterflies around here.

My brothers come home from the baseball game. They are covered with sweat and dirt. Grandpa says they got to scrub up. Kory, my middle brother, sticks his tongue out at me, and I stick up my middle finger behind Grandpa's head. Kory giggles and goes off into the bathroom. I turn up my hearing aids and listen real hard. Sounds like they're squabbling again. I'm real glad I'm not a brother. They have it hard when there's more than one. They have to fight for everything.

I have it easy because I'm a girl. They don't want girl things so they leave me alone for the most part. Sometimes they want to play rough with Fuzzy, but they know enough not to tease him for too long. My little brother Karl got bit on the wrist once, but that was because he kept pulling Fuzzy's tail real hard, thinking he could pull it off like a dead squirrel's. Dad was so mad at Karl. That was the first time I heard Dad call anyone stupid. Karl couldn't use his left hand for three weeks.

Mom wanted to give Fuzzy away to someone else, but Fuzzy just kept his head real low and stayed behind me whenever he was in the house. Fuzzy always stays away from Karl no matter what.

I told Mom that Fuzzy was my best friend.

She changed her mind. But Karl never touches Fuzzy. Ever.

Suddenly Fuzzy scoots off to the front door. That means someone's at the door.

We all follow him. I peek out the kitchen window to see whose car it is. It's ours. Mom's opening up a wheelchair next to Grandma's seat in the car, and Dad's lifting Grandma from the car onto her wheelchair.

Dad hollers my brothers out of the house, and he gives them a suitcase each from the trunk. Grandma's been away from this house for almost two months. I didn't like the hospital, and she didn't either. She told me so herself. But I came every day with flowers from the fields near Logan Park. Mostly I made lots of get-well cards, and she let me tape them all over her wall. Mom says that Grandma has to exercise her legs even if they can't walk anymore. She says that it's good for her blood.

Grandpa hasn't stepped outside yet. He hasn't come to the hospital for two months. Mom told me not to ask him anything about Grandma because he gets mad real easy. He turns away and goes back into the living room. It's not nice what he's doing.

I follow him. "Grandma's home. Come on." I tug at his hand.

He pulls away and says nothing. He presses his remote control. The volume of the TV goes up so loud even I can hear it.

I go back to the front door, and Mom and my brothers are standing in the kitchen. Dad is pushing Grandma through the front door into the kitchen. It's so strange to see her in a wheelchair here, 'specially in this kitchen. I remember how she always stood next to the stove, stirring hot cereal or waiting for the molasses cookies to finish baking or chopping carrots on the counter. She never liked to sit still like Grandpa. She always liked me to help. She said I was her best helper, even better than Mom when she was a little girl.

Grandma looks up at me and holds her arms out. "My baby."

I hug her. It's strange to hold her like this, because she always felt bigger than me. Now she's a bit shorter than me. Very strange. Fuzzy wags his tail, so I lift his front legs onto her lap. She hugs Fuzzy, which makes him happily wag his tail. She likes Fuzzy, too.

Fuzzy gets off and sniffs her wheelchair. Grandma starts to push herself through the dining room and the living room. Karl rushes to help push her, but she waves him away. She goes on, but the doorway is a little narrow for her arms hanging over her wheels. She grips the doorway and glides over into the dining room.

We are all behind her, watching her navigate around the dining room table. There isn't enough room for her to move around real easy. Dad said that we might have to help move furniture around when she got home, but we are supposed to wait and see how much room she needs first.

Grandpa says nothing. He don't look at her at all. Just keeps watching TV. I can't believe he's so mean.

She says something. I can hear her, but I can't understand everything she says because I can't lipread her from behind.

Grandpa says something and shrugs his shoulders.

I hate him now. I never thought he was such a meanie.

Grandma turns around and wheels forward to the kitchen.

Dad and Mom and my brothers are looking at Grandpa with shock on their faces. Fuzzy breaks past me, pounces on Grandma's lap, and tries to lick the tears off her face. Normally Grandma wouldn't allow him to do that, but Grandpa's so mean, and Fuzzy's so nice. She says, "Maybe we should make a pie now?"

In the kitchen, I sit with Grandma, picking over the raspberries. Mom sits with us, helping out too. Dad's in the living room with Grandpa. I can hear them even if the door's closed. Grandma and Mom say nothing while they listen. Sometimes they raise eyebrows at each other and trade glances with each berry dropping into a big ceramic bowl. Fuzzy's watching me from under the kitchen table. It's his favorite place in Grandma's house because everybody has to go through the kitchen before going anywhere else in the house, and he likes to see who's coming in and who's going out.

My brothers are sitting on the stairs leading down to the kitchen. They are real quiet, too. I imagine them listening real close to what Dad and Grandpa are saying, but I can't understand all of the words.

Mom clears the table, wipes it clean, and sprinkles the flour all over instead of on the counter. Grandma's about to roll the pie dough. At first I was upset in the hospital when I saw her in the wheelchair, but when Dad explained to me that it helped her to get around, like my hearing aids helped me to get around, I didn't feel so bad. She laughed when I asked to go riding on her "chairbike."

Suddenly Grandpa comes into the kitchen and looks at her. He says, "What good are you if you're like this?" He clutches his hand into the bowl of raspberries and flings them all over the floor. His hand drips like blood as he steps outside.

Dad shouts something at him. I know it's a bad word because he uses it when he's real angry.

Grandma lugs the bowl of raspberries and swings it at the window in front of her. It's an old window so it shatters easy and makes a huge noise. The bowl falls over outside on the yard. She yells, "Coward! Coward!"

I look down at Fuzzy. His tail is right between his legs. I go under the table and pet him, just to let him know he's all right. Some pieces of glass have fallen on him. I pull them out real careful and drop them next to the bigger pieces. I don't want Fuzzy to bleed.

My brothers are already scooping the red mess off the floor with paper towels. For once they're not fighting. I hold Fuzzy's collar so he won't go sniffing for raspberries and hurt his feet from the broken glass.

Kory beckons me to come out from under the table. The floor's clean.

By then Dad has gone out of the house. Mom holds me real tight. I keep looking at Grandma. I can't help it. She looks older than I remember.

Grandma says, "I'm sorry—I'm so sorry about your pie."

"I can pick some more if you want."

After a minute, she nods at last.

Fuzzy and I are off with my bucket. This time we'll find the biggest raspberries, and Grandma will make the best pie in the whole world. *Ever*.

K

"Let's try it again. The sound."

"No."

"Please. Feel my *k*."

"I don't wanna touch your neck. I'm fourteen, okay?"

"Look—look at me. Please."

"Why aren't my hearig friens talking to you? Even my teachers can't undersand wha they say half the time."

"You need to do this if you want to graduate. This is an individualized class."

"Oh, so you're gonna grade me on the *quality* of my speech. Do you also grade how people who use crutches walk? The *quality* of their walk?"

In college, when I was studying Ling's theory on speech production, no one ever warned me about students like Frank. As an intern at the New York League for the Hard of Hearing and at a mainstreamed high school program in Salt Lake City, I encountered deaf and hard of hearing people whose speech was impossible to understand. Others, who were mostly hard of hearing or who had speech therapists training them right after their diagnosis, were a joy to work with, because they already understood the importance of good speech.

"Frank, you're hearing-impaired."

"Oh, great."

"What?"

"Hi."

"I don't understand."

"Hearig-impaired. H-i. I'm a Hi with a big happy smile stretchig from hearig aid to hearig aid. I'm a Hi-Ha. Get it?"

"Oh, eh. I see."

"I'm not a Hi."

"All right. So you don't have a problem with yourself?"

"No."

"Then why do you still need me?"

"I *don't* need you, lady."

"You're fourteen years old."

"Why won't you tell me how old you are?"

"Because I'm older than you."

"Oh, no. It's because you think you're betta than me. You're hearig."

"I only want to help you."

"People like you make me stick."

"Frank! You're very rude."

"I never assed to have your hands all over my neck."

"You ... I'm flabbergasted. Really."

"The only weason why I want to perfect my *k* is to say: Fuc*k* you. Yeah."

The classroom is a home that Frank would never return to, yet it breathes like a ghost in the deepest recesses of his dreams. It is a room of four walls, often with large windows that show the seasons gradually changing while he learns new words and sentences and concepts each day; the memory of being young and small is indelibly imprinted on his brain. The ceilings are very high and the suspended fluorescent rods are nothing like the lights at home, but as the days go by, he stops noticing the light until the janitor replaces them.

The classroom is a different world where Frank sees his own niche in the pecking order and bigger scheme of things. He isn't sure what the bigger scheme of things is supposed to be, but he senses his place in it all over again the second he steps into the classroom where there are six others just like him, but with varying speaking abilities. He walks by the vast bulletin boards, mapped with colorful construction paper and cutouts as his teacher nods acknowledgment. This fall he would learn the days of the week, months of the year, and names of seasons.

His teacher and parents had already decided a long time before that Frank would be eventually mainstreamed with his hearing peers. His superior speaking and listening skills meant success, guaranteed.

"How was your weekend?"

"BFD. Wha? You know, I've been thikig."

"I've had a discussion with your parents."

"Yeah?"

"Don't you want to hear the rest of it?"

"They told me everythig."

"If they did, you wouldn't be here."

"Then *you* lied."

"Maybe they never sat you down for dinner to talk about this."

". . . ."

"Frank? Aren't you going to say something?"

". . . ."

"Don't tell me you've chosen not to speak. Don't be so absurd. How can anyone *not* speak and succeed?"

All of Frank's speech therapists were deified by both his teachers and parents, who shook their heads in amazement over Frank's progress. His speech therapist's kingdom was the half-circled table in the back of the hearing-impaired classroom. His parents clasped their hands gratefully with his speech therapist's, as if she'd saved the world—always theirs and never his. With her gentle admonishments and an occasional slap against his hands if Frank pointed to something instead of using his voice, he was left with a feeling of shrinking in spite of his growing body. Of course, he was too young to realize the ramifications of this behavior modification then. By the time he finally read up on Deaf culture at the public library, at the age of fifteen, it was too late to blame any single hearing person for the depth of dissociation in his life.

"Frank! Shut up and listen to me right now."

"Why? You don't have to live with this shitty voice. *I* do."

"Oh, no. The world has to hear you."

"Then why aren't they hearing our *sssss*ibilant screams? Not well-modulated enough and not from the somach, huh?"

"You have great potential. Don't waste it on anger."

"Don't you *ever* stop and think how you'd feel if you had a stranger forcing you to talk in ways you don't undersand?"

"But—but, Frank, you're *speaking*. You can talk almost like anyone else. Most people can understand you."

"Sometimes I swear I'll shut my voice off and let it wus like an old wagon wheel out in the fiels."

"Frank, I can't believe—look, you're very intelligent. You should know better than to fall prey to the politics of ..."

"Oooh, you're sayig that speech therapy ain't political?"

"Isn't."

"What have I learn from speech? Let me coun the ways I love speech therapy."

"I don't want to hear them."

"You're upset. I'm thrilled to see all that emotion in your face. Ready for the ways I love—"

"Get it over with."

". . . ."

"You know I don't know sign language."

". . . ."

"What's that supposed to mean?"

"I feel so abnormal when I have to thin about the fuc*k*in' *k*. I feel so infewior when I have to repeat twenty times what you've said only once. I feel so stupid when I try to make small tal and even stupider when they laugh and unnerstand all my dirty words. I'm not a normal freag."

"But Frank. You have no reason to be bitter. Your speech is so much better than most deaf people's."

"Oh, and that means I will be betta off than they are? And I'm supposed to compare myself with them so I can preten I'm betta than them?"

What else could I say to Frank that would make him see that I'm not as evil as the Deaf community likes to make me seem? My job is not about politics; I just teach deaf people *and* brain-damaged hearing people how to speak properly. *That's all.*

Yet when I tell my friends that I am a speech therapist for deaf students, some of them seem surprised that I don't know sign language. The Deaf community may have scored a big victory against people like me right there, but many hearing educators still find it hard to resist the notion of enabling deaf people to speak. It's like Helen Keller all over again.

In such difficult cases like Frank's, I'm always advised to marshal the attention of the people who matter most to him so that he'll get to see the folly of his ideas. The hearing world doesn't care for some of the politics that go on inside the Deaf community; they just want to feel they can *understand* their deaf children. It's so ridiculous, the way they have to force their politics on us.

"Your father asked me to work with you, that's why."

"Oh, come on. He knows I'll never be like him. What's the big deal?"

"Let's just get to work, okay?"

"Testy, testy, aren'tcha."

"We'll work on *s* and *st* today."

"Suff it."

"You really have a hearing problem. You don't hear anyone but yourself."

"That's cool."

"I don't know how your parents can talk with you with this attitude of yours."

". . . ."

"Why aren't you saying anything? Don't use your hands."

". . . ."

"What?"

"I have wights, you know."

Years before, when the possibility that their baby son might be deaf occurred to them for the first time, Frank's parents talked about everything but this: The Deaf people with whom they had come into brief contact seemed overly cheerful, as if they wanted all the others around them to forget they were different at all. His parents saw them all at a distance, hauling groceries, sorting mail, and cranking the linotype presses. The fate that befell their son was horrifying. In those early years of testing Frank's hearing, outfitting him with hearing aids, setting him up for early speech training—the cycle of activities to make sure that Frank was caught up with his hearing peers was just endless. And horrifying: There was no other word for it.

So the notion of their son—once a young deaf boy with no distinguishable facial features—becoming a doctor would've been too much for most hearing people, let alone his parents. Yet one day his parents would be overwhelmingly proud when he graduated with honors, *summa cum laude,* and a pristine MD in school psychiatry. But they would never know exactly why he had become so driven to accomplish so much with internships, papers, and conferences; if they did, their hearts would be broken all over again.

"Let me try again. The sign."

". . . ."

"What?"

". . . ."

"I'm supposed to turn off my voice. You know I can't."

". . . ."

"What's that? You can talk to me."

". . . ."

"It's a . . . *p*? No. Oh. *K*."

". . . ."

"Now what?"

". . . ."

"Can't you speak for once? And save us some time?"

". . . ."

"You know, you can be so ..."

". . . ."

"This is not funny! At all!"

When I reviewed the new Individualized Education Plan for Frank's speech therapy in front of Frank, his mother, and my boss, I was furious. *I* had to learn signs. Of course, more and more speech therapists have to deal with the eventuality of learning signs due to the varying educational approaches for Deaf students across the country, but the difference between deaf people who speak and Deaf people who speak and sign, is very noticeable, even to those who don't know "deaf speech."

Worse yet, in our next session, he made me feel like such an idiot because I kept flubbing my fingerspelling. Just when the bell rang, he couldn't resist using his voice: "Now you know how I feel about speech therapis who humilate me."

I swear I wanted to hit him, but he was already gone.

*

"You don't know just how blessed you are."

"Try explaining that to my parens."

"They love you. You know that."

"Really? You're no differen from my parens. You people still want to believe that maybe if a disabled guy had the *right* operation, the *right* crutch, the *right* therapis, he'd do the foxtrot perfectly. The story of his life. And mine. Just thin about it."

"Wait. You're leaving now?"

". . . ."

I didn't go to Frank's high school graduation, where he sign-interpreted one of the songs. I just wanted to *forget* the gestures he'd made in the classroom doorway before he let the door close on us alone: He crossed his big hands around his throat, pretending to look deathly ill, and then his aimless eyes suddenly latched on some imaginary Deaf person in the classroom. His hands slowly fell away from his neck and began signing things I couldn't follow. He kissed the top of his fists and caressed his wounded hands lovingly before outstretching his arms in an emphatic freedom gesture.

Of those days when he was forced to speak, Frank vividly remembers his other six classmates in the hearing-impaired classroom. Even though a great many years have gone by, he remembers them all with frightening clarity, for they were the first to make him aware that he wasn't alone with his hearing aids.

Together they scissored out pictures and fought over broken crayons and played outside on the seesaw, completely oblivious to the fact that they were all cut off from a comfortable language of their own. And so Frank and his small family of deaf classmates constantly wondered why something was so terribly amiss when they'd spent so many hours together. They knew each other's exterior actions, but never anything of each other's interior lives.

Oh, yes. Frank would change all of that, and then maybe for all those Deaf kids looking up to him, he would make them feel more at home with themselves.

THE FINER THINGS

Michael is wandering the circular hallways of the Hirschhorn Gallery of Art when he notices an older man with a thick blond beard, wearing a pair of olive corduroys and burgundy Weejuns. Michael looks away, wishing he didn't always have to explore art museums alone and be pursued by one man or another on Saturday afternoons. He knows other men seem to admire his own rust-colored beard and the shape of his ass, but his lover Ted had said he could never be patient enough to sit and stare at paintings the way Michael did. He moves on to the next sculpture, which appears to be made of long copper toothpicks; it looks torn between two skewered fences. He doesn't note the name of the sculptor; he is feeling somewhat hot and hard because that man keeps glancing back now and then; he thinks, *If he smiles again, I'm cooked.* The year is 1988.

He turns his hearing aids back on, just in case the man approaches him; for when alone, he has no need for sound. He always forgets how loud the groans of the Metrobus can be when it passes, or how incessantly babbling a crowd of people can be. Besides, silence helps him concentrate on the painting in front of him and ignore the squeals of children pointing out this and that on the walls.

The next time he looks, the man smiles openly. He chuckles somewhat at Michael's embarrassment and strides over. "What do you think of this sculpture?"

Michael looks up, surprised by how tall the man is, and how hazel his eyes are. Their color reminds him of golden maple leaves turning brown. "I'm sorry?" he asks as he turns up the volume on his hearing aids.

"Oh." The man points to his own ear. "Can you hear me?"

"Yes. Just say it again."

"I was asking, What do you think of this work?"

"Oh." Michael looks at it. "It doesn't make any sense."

"Then what are you doing here?" The man chuckles.

Michael drops his shoulders. "I don't know."

"Were you looking or ... ?"

"I have a lover."

"He doesn't try to understand you? Or this?"

Michael laughs nervously, thinking, *Who does he think he is? I don't need anyone telling me what to do.*

"Come on now." The man places a hand on Michael's shoulder. "What's your name?"

"Michael."

"Ah, Michael. I'm Alec." As they shake hands, Michael notices how moist their palms are. "Mind if we go outside? I need to smoke."

From their bench, Michael can see the panorama of tourists walking toward the Washington Monument to see the cherry blossoms on the Tidal Basin. In two months he will graduate with a bachelor's degree in graphic arts from Gallaudet University; he's not sure where in this city he could find a job in his field.

"Michael, I don't know if you've seen me around before, but I've noticed you."

"You have? Where?"

"Up at the Corcoran. You seem to like postcard reproductions of Caravaggio and Raphael a tremendous lot."

Michael's jaw drops.

"Yes," he chuckles. "And I was so pleased to see you again, because it's not often I see someone so cute standing there so patiently in front of some painting." He inhales from his cigarette. "Tell me, what are you studying now?"

"Graphic arts at Gallaudet."

"Wasn't that great, with all that coverage on the student protest for a Deaf president recently? I'll bet you were thrilled when King Jordan won."

"Yeah. He's still trying to get used to being the top dog on campus. So we just move on and do what we must do."

He shakes his head. "But don't you ever study art itself? Literature? Things like that ... My God, you have such a fine nose. Would you know how I'd paint that? I'd paint it simply like ..."

"Like van Eyck?" Michael is not even sure if his pronunciation is correct.

"Yes! But tell me, why are you taking graphic arts when you should be at the Corcoran?"

"I don't know." Michael points to his ears. "Reason enough for you?"

"No." He exhales smoke meditatively. "I'm trying to think of any great artist who was deaf, and all I can think of is Beethoven. You know his work?"

"Never heard his music." Michael shrugs.

"Oh, you must hear him! What about Mozart?"

"Who?"

"What are they teaching you over there? Andy Warhol?"

"No ... but I happen to like some of his Pop Art."

"What he's doing is a total insult to the standards of art! It's not Pop Art, it's Slop Art!"

Michael is surprised to see that anyone could be so vehement over Warhol, or over any artist for that matter. "Why?"

"Now all the young artists think they don't need mastery of any craft to pass for art, true and genuine art! It's supposed to take years and years before someone dares to call himself an artist. You see, I'm not terribly fond of modern or contemporary art."

"I guess I'm different from you." Michael is surprised at how much he wants to push Alec a little more—and he is really a total stranger, come to think of it—just to hear more of his opinions. "I like modern art."

"Watch what terms you use. You just don't throw them around like—"

"Like Tiddlywinks?"

He laughs. "Yes! I hope you do know the difference between modern and contemporary art?"

"Modern art is by those who worked and died in this century; contemporary is by those who are still working and living in this century."

"Ahh." Alec smiles. "Shall we have dinner in Georgetown? My treat."

As Alec ushers him into L'Escargot and leads him to a table near the back of the restaurant, Michael wonders what his lover Ted would think of all this. Michael feels awkward among the many tables covered with immaculately white tablecloths and so many wineglasses with triangularly folded napkins resting neatly inside. They walk past cream-colored candles in shiny brass holders waiting to be lit on empty tables; Michael is not sure what to do with his old denim jacket. Alec takes it without saying a word, hangs it on the coat hook behind him, and gestures that he sit opposite him.

Alec lights another cigarette and says, "I know the owner so I get the best table here. You like it?"

Michael looks around, and looks at himself, even more embarrassed over his appearance. He is wearing an old shirt, Levi's, and a pair of black Converse basketball sneakers. "I—I've never been in a fancy place like this."

"No one ever uses the adjective 'fancy' anymore. This is an *upscale* place for people who know how to appreciate the finer things of life."

"The finer things of life?"

"Yes. Great art. Great food. Great music. Listen." Alec leans over to one side. "Can you hear that?"

Michael turns up his hearing aids again. The music seems florid with piano keys twinkling among violins. "A little."

"That's Ravel. He's a French composer. Have you ever heard 'Bolero'?"

"What?" He feels embarrassed.

"Michael. Do you want to learn about the finer things of life? Don't you and your lover want to live around here? Look, where are the galleries?"

"Dupont Circle. And sometimes Adams Morgan. Where else?"

"Right. Don't you want to live like these people?"

Michael remembers walking the streets of Dupont Circle and Georgetown during his first year in Washington. He peered at the walls behind lit windows; they seemed always filled with hardcover books and inevitably a painting or two on the opposite wall. He dreamed often of taking his cold and wet shoes off these nights, wriggling his toes in the crackling heat of their fireplaces, and poring over all those art books. He finally says, "I don't know any Deaf people who live like you."

The waiter comes around. "*Et quelque chose à boire, pêut-etre?*"

"I don't know." Michael looks helplessly at Alec.

"*Je pense q'un boutaille de votre Bordeaux préférée—pêut-etre 1978—fait du bien, n'est-ce pas?*"

"*Oui, monsieur.*"

When the waiter leaves, Michael leans over. "What was that?"

Alec laughs. "You are going to taste some wonderful wine, my dear. Now, tell me." He opens his menu. "Have you ever tried *escargots*?"

"What?" Michael is still dazzled by the prices on the menu, and the fact that none of the French titles explain what the dishes contain. Worse yet, he doesn't know how to pronounce anything in French.

"Look." Alec's fingernail points to the *premiers plats* section and drops down to the word *escargots*.

"Never heard of them."

"What? You must try a few. They're delicate, but oh, so delicate."

"But what are they?"

"Snails cooked in a buttery sauce."

"Snails? Do you eat the shells too?"

"Oh, God, no. Just wait and see." He chuckles. "Mind if I order what I think would be an exquisite introduction to French gourmet cooking?"

"To French what?"

"Gourmet cooking."

"What's that?"

"Haven't you ever heard of 'gourmet'?"

"No. Could you spell it out?"

"G-o-u-r-m-e-t."

"Gour-met?"

"No. You say it the French way. Gour-may."

"Gour-may?"

"Yes. Gourmet."

"Gourmet."

"There. You got it. Don't you have some special teacher showing you how to say all those wonderful words?"

"No. I never met a speech therapist who was into gourmet cooking."

He laughs, but stops. "Are you really that deaf?"

"Sometimes."

"But you don't seem to need sign language."

"I can't live without it."

"Why not?"

"It's just a part of me." He hated speech therapy even more when he saw how much easier it was to converse with his hands. It felt so natural, so of course.

"But what about this artistic part of you?"

"That's the hearing part of me, I suppose."

"The what part of you?"

"Hearing. You're hearing. I'm Deaf."

"Oh, so that's what Deaf people call normal people—"

"Hearing people are not normal when they think they're better than Deaf people."

Alec's face flickers briefly as he extinguishes his cigarette into an ashtray. "I didn't mean to suggest ... I'm very sorry if I offended you."

"It's all right. Really."

"You know what just occurred to me? No finer thing is ever normal, and so I intend to banish that word from my vocabulary right now. But you must remember, if you want to appreciate the finer things of life, you can't bend so low you forget what art's all about."

They watch the waiter open the Bordeaux and pour a sparkling trickle of wine into Alec's glass. He sniffs and tastes it, swishing the wine in his mouth for what seems minutes. He nods; the waiter pours it into both their glasses and leaves. Alec pats the back of Michael's hand and indicates they should both hold their glasses up in the air. "Cheers."

"Cheers?"

"It's a standard greeting. A toast."

"Oh. Cheers."

"Ahh," Alec smiles after he sips from his glass. "Just superb."

Michael sips. The wine tingles along his tastebuds, and down his throat. He feels slightly hot, as if in a fever but not quite, and a flush comes over his ears.

"What do you think?"

"I don't know."

"You must learn to determine and give opinions. An opinionated man is much more intriguing. And that's the point of art."

"What is the point of art?"

"A well-crafted statement, pure and simple. Tell me, what do you think of the wine?"

Michael thinks what would be an appropriate statement, a good opinion: "It's light as a summer rain."

Alec claps his hands together and holds them to his lips. "Michael. That is beautiful. It makes me wonder why you're with a lover who doesn't share the things you want to do the most."

"I don't know. He's DeafBlind."

"Deaf ... Blind? Oh. So he can't see art the same way you do."

"No. But I think he sees it in a very different way than we do. People rely too much on their ears and eyes. He relies on his nose, and he could tell you just about anything by smelling."

"But what does his nose have to do with art?"

"Isn't art supposed to be a complete experience ... ?"

"I wish ... Oh. I see what you mean. The nose is the most underrated of all our senses."

"Right."

"Well, I hope he appreciates your beautiful nose. In any case, great art should inspire all of our senses."

Michael feels his body tensing; he somehow feels Alec will be able to ease that vague yearning inside him. There's got to be something more to life than just getting a job, a lover, and a nice apartment.

The waiter returns for their order. As Michael sips his wine, he tries to lipread the French flitting back and forth. Their voices seem like strains of a melody he has to hear more of. Alec smiles at him as he indicates the various dishes Michael should try. "*Merci bien.*"

"What was that?"

"We were speaking French."

"I know, but what was that last thing you said?"

"*Merci bien?* That was 'thank you' in French."

"How do you say it?"

"*Merci bien.*"

"*Merci* bine?"

"No. *Merci bien.*"

"*Merci bien?*"

"Now you'll be able to thank Pierre when the meal is over."

"Pear?"

"No. Pierre. French for 'Peter.'"

"Oh, Pierre."

After a sip, Alec leans forward. "So it seems you know a tremendous lot, but you've never heard things pronounced ..."

"Yes." Michael is pleased that someone else—a virtual stranger—could deduce that much. "What do you do for a living?"

"I write essays on art and film, and I review biographies, that sort of thing, for a lot of magazines."

"Which ones?"

"Oh, you'd never have heard of them. They're just avant-garde."

"They're what?"

"Avant-garde. Different."

"I don't understand."

"I'll spell it, okay. A-v-a-n-t g-a-r-d-e."

"Oh. That's how you say it?"

"Yes. Avant-garde."

"Avant-garde?"

"You got it right." Alec pauses. "You ever hear of *The New Yorker*?"

He looks about, a little lost.

"Michael, you can't not have heard of it!"

He feels hotly humiliated. No one told him he should read that; there were always so many things he wanted to read.

"Oh, you must read it! A lot of opinionated people write stuff for it every week. You'd love it. Look, I'll get you a copy."

"You don't have to—"

"Nonsense. Not enough people know how to appreciate art, and you are dying to soak it all up. You've given me a mission."

"A what?"

"A mission. 'I'm going to show you things you never dreamed existed.' Like that? That's from *Auntie Mame*."

"*Auntie Mame*?"

"Don't tell me you've never seen it."

"Is it closed-captioned?"

"I'm sorry?"

"I have this box on my TV that brings out the hidden captions of the dialogue if it's closed-captioned."

"Why should you worry about that when you can understand me just fine?"

"Movies are not made to be lipread. You are."

"Well, Rosalind Russell is wonderful. You really must see it sometime. Oh, I can't believe this. There's a million worlds awaiting you. I'll show them all to you, if you want."

"What kinds of things?" Michael feels a little tipsy. The wine is very good, he thinks. He must remember to ask Alec the name of it so he can ask for it the next time he goes out with Ted.

"Do you ever listen to music?"

"Sometimes."

"Rock music?"

"Yeah."

"Oh, dear. You don't know what you're missing."

"What am I missing?"

"Worlds!" Alec lights another cigarette. "It's a shame you don't live with a lover who could be teaching the things you really want to know."

"But I love him. Very much." Michael lowers his eyes.

Alec places his hand on Michael's. "I'm sorry. To whom do you like to listen?"

"The Pretenders, The Police, The Who, The Beatles, The Beach Boys."

"At least there's still hope for you. You like classic contemporary music. That can translate well into classical music."

"But I don't know if I can hear the quiet stuff."

"Don't worry. That kind of appreciation comes over a long time."

The waiter places two tiny plates of grilled *escargots* between the two men.

Michael says, "*Merci bien.*"

"*Je suis étonné—votre français est parfait!*" The waiter looks bewildered by Michael.

Alec laughs. "*Il ne connaît encore que 'Merci bien.'*"

The waiter looks relieved and leaves.

"What did you say?"

"I told him your French is limited to 'Thank you.'"

"*Merci bien.* Oh, I speak such bad French."

Alec laughs as he takes his tiny escargot fork and pitches the tiny ball of meat out of the snail's shell. "You go on, try it." He dips it into the sauce. "Mm-hmm. They did it just right, as usual."

Michael looks apprehensively at it before he imitates Alec in dipping it into the sauce. He feels funny eating snail, but he is surprised at how good it tastes in his mouth. He is disappointed that there are only six snails left, and that each shell could contain only so little.

"Ahh. Now sip some wine. See how it affects your taste."

Michael's tongue feels suddenly bathed in a trickle of warmth. "It just feels different."

"That's the miracle of a great wine. You feel different."

"What?"

"Don't worry. You'll understand everything, all of what translates into the finer things of life. Here, have some more." He indicates the *escargots*. "You have so much more to learn. You have the nose for it."

"Stop talking about my nose!"

"I can't help it, it's so perfect." Alec gazes at Michael past the swaying candlelight. "May I touch it?"

As Michael feels Alec's finger tracing the ridges of his nose, he thinks about his lover. He realizes with a sudden pulse of pain that he and Ted have stopped exploring each other's bodies. When they'd first met, their hands and tongues were absolutely carnivorous; now they just focus on their genitals.

"Why do you look so sad?"

"Oh, it's nothing."

"It's him, isn't it?"

"Yes," he says with a sigh. "It's just not the same."

"People change. No one likes it when that happens. But change—that's the best and secret ingredient for great art."

"Secret what?"

"In-*gree*-di-ent."

"I'm sorry?"

"I-n-g-r-e-d-i-e-n-t."

"Oh. The stuff that goes into food?"

He nods. "Michael, I take it you want to be an artist."

"Me? An artist? In what?"

"Anything you want. You should show me your portfolio sometime."

"Well, I've done some collages ..."

They look up as the waiter brings one dish after another to their table. "*Bon appétit!*"

"*Merci bien.*"

Alec tries not to laugh. "Did you truly understand what he said?"

"No. I just said 'thank you.' I mean, what else can I say?"

"You're funny." Alec holds up his glass. "*Bon appétit.*"

"*Bon appétit?*"

"You got it."

As they sip their wines, Michael thinks again of Ted, who must be wondering now why he hasn't come home yet. How could he explain something like Alec to Ted, or to any of his Deaf friends? They've never cared all that much about art; the looks on their faces loosen when they can talk about other topics like Marlee Matlin or Gallaudet's new administration.

Michael tries a little bit of everything on Alec's plate and cleans his own plate. Everything is astonishingly delicious—he has never been so in love with any food before. As he watches Alec sign the credit card slip, he thinks, *I must go to Paris and try more of their food.* His stomach's fullness feels nice.

They walk in the twilight down to a magazine and book shop on M Street, where Alec pulls a copy of *The New Yorker*. "This is for you."

Michael looks at the pastel colorings of its Roz Chast cover; he recognizes the magazine now, but he's never read the inside. "*Merci bien.*"

Alec laughs as he shakes his pack of cigarette for another one. "So you live off 16th Street?" He looks in the distance, where M Street splinters into Pennsylvania Avenue; if they walk a few blocks further over the P Street bridge, they'll be in Dupont Circle.

"I envy your lover. I really do."

"No, you shouldn't. I envy you, that you're able to know so much."

"Is it really that hard for Deaf people like you?"

"What do you mean?"

"To appreciate art."

"Well, there's Deaf culture. I suppose that's a different kind of art."

"Yes, it must be. Sign language has its own beauty ... But don't you want to learn more about art?"

"Well. I'm afraid of becoming so hearing I'll forget that I'm a Deaf person."

"I don't think you'll forget. It just colors everything you do, that's all. When Beethoven became deaf, he wrote his greatest music ... Oh

God. I do want to kiss your nose."

"Not here."

"Do we have to go all the way to Dupont Circle just so we can kiss?"

Michael turns pink under the streetlight; they are ready to cross the bridge toward the subway station. "I've never had an affair before, and I don't intend to get into the habit."

"Michael, have you ever been to New York?"

"No."

"You must. Tell you what. If I could take you up there next weekend, would you go?"

"What could I tell Ted?"

"Lie a little."

"I can't. I don't like to lie."

"You cannot be an artist without knowing what New York—or any large city filled with open-minded artists like you—is like. You must meet as many New Yorkers as you can and hang around with people who appreciate the same things you do. Having them all in one place like New York makes creativity a lot easier than here in Washington."

"Then why do you live here?"

"The rent here is a hell of a lot cheaper. I go up to New York at least twice a month. Would you like to go? I could introduce you to a few people."

"Are they stuck up? That's what I've heard."

"Whoever told you that? If they weren't friendly with people like you, they'd be out of business. They need something fresh, something original to stay in business."

"Oh. I never thought of that. But some galleries here don't seem to like having me around."

"They're always looking for people with money. You know, I could stand here for hours and be perfectly happy if I could be talking with you like this."

"Don't lie to me." He grins. "You said you wanted to kiss my nose."

"Oh yes, that too. That would make me so very happy. May I?"

Michael glances around. "I don't know. It has to be somewhere else."

"You're welcome to my place." Alec kisses the tip of his index finger as if to say, *Allow me to kiss you—please.*

"Could I have your phone number?"

"Gladly!" His hands dart in and out of his pockets until he plucks out his card. "So are you thinking about coming to New York?"

Michael nods as he reads the card: ALEXANDER A. JONSON.

"Would you understand me on the telephone?"

"You've been so easy to lipread so far, I can't imagine having a problem."

He watches the passing cars before he fixes his eyes on Michael's. "Can I have your number?"

"I don't think it's a good idea right now."

"Well, all right. I understand. When can I see you again?"

"I'll call you."

"You're not one of those people who says that and never calls?"

"Alec. I told you, I've never had an affair before."

"It's not an affair. Yet."

"I don't know if I can sleep with you."

"You're still in love with him?"

"Well, that's the problem. I don't know."

"Let's walk over to Dupont Circle."

In front of Ted's pink apartment building, Michael asks, "What time is it now?"

"Almost ten."

"Ted won't like this."

"Oh. I just don't have the heart to ask you again ..."

"My nose?" Michael rolls his eyes upward in exasperation.

"Yes."

Alec leans over and kisses his nose furtively and quickly. "You know that's not enough for me." He slips a hand into his front pocket and pushes up his erection. "Now I have a problem here. Please." He sighs. "Call me."

Ted is already sleeping when Michael comes in. He strips and slips into the cold place beside him. Ted reaches for the light and turns it back on. "Where all-day where?"

Michael puts his hands under Ted's so he can read his signs.

"Me-look-around H-i-r-s-c-h-h-o-r-n Museum, me-meet g-a-l-l-e-r-y o-w-n-e-r want see my work, maybe me-join ride New-York."

"New-York dangerous awful place, too-many muggings, won't g-o."

"Most artists live where other then?"

"Here. You here."

"I-f you don't-want go New-York, me-go."

"Money where?"

"G-a-l-l-e-r-y o-w-n-e-r money have."

"O-h. You-like money? Himself gay?"

"Gay not-matter, want-want help me important."

"Slept-with-him finish?"

"Don't-like talk. Me-thought you trust me."

"Me-48, you-22. You-young, don't-know do-do, horny a-l-l time, don't-know how control, too-many people dying AIDS now."

"FINISH!" Michael signs and yells at the same time. He leaps out of the bed and stares at Ted signing to the air in front of him. He wants to weep because Ted doesn't know where Michael is in their tiny apartment, and he wonders who'd want to take care of Ted if he leaves. He pulls his clothes back on and signs into Ted's hands, "You not-understand what me-need life, my life."

"You young. Of-course."

"Not-like your-use age excuse. You-want me-stay here, like jail. You not-want understand passion."

"My fault that?"

"We talk-talk same-same. Enough. Me-stay-with friend tonight. Me-come-back tomorrow."

"Me-thought you l-o-v-e love me."

Michael feels his eyes burn. "Love too but don't-know i-f enough for you."

At a pay phone outside, he dials Alec's number and turns up the volume on his hearing aid. He hears his answering machine, and then suddenly, a click. "Hello?"

"Alec?"

"Michael! Are you all right?"

"I need a place to stay tonight."

"You need money for a cab?"

"No. I need to walk a bit first, just to clear my head."

"Absolutely."

Michael walks to Alec's basement apartment on O Street, not far from the Dumbarton Oaks Gardens, and rings the bell. Alec is wearing a black-and-red velvet bathrobe as he opens the door to let Michael in.

He looks around and sees shelves of books everywhere. He looks at the shimmering parquet floor and treads across it gingerly as if it is a glass sheet waiting to break. "Michael, let me take your jacket. You can sleep on the sofa if you like."

"Thanks. *Merci bien.*"

Alec grins slowly. "Do you want to talk about it?"

"No. Not tonight."

"Ah, I see. Do you want some tea or something?"

"Oh no. *Merci bien* anyway."

"You don't know how hilarious you can be. Oh, Michael ..."

"I'm not in the mood for heavy talk tonight."

"Okay." Alec brings out designer sheets and a goose-down comforter. "It's kind of cold here, but you should be warm enough. I think you'd be a lot warmer next to me, of course."

"No, *merci bien.*"

As Michael lies there and watches the occasional headlights sweep through the front window, he gazes across these books on the shelves, wondering what kind of things he would learn, and what kind of person he would be if he could learn all the things Alec knows. Would he be so different that Deaf friends wouldn't know what to do with him? Would they accuse him of being too hearing? Perhaps life would be easier for him in New York; he'd met at various Deaf parties some truly nice people who lived there. After all, he would be graduating in two months.

As he turns off the bathroom light, he sees Alec sleeping. He's left his bedroom door open. He steps in and notices that Alec's pectorals and lower arms are covered with feathery hairs.

"Alec?" He whispers.

His eyes do not flicker. He comes closer to the edge of the bed, catches the scant moonlight illuminating Alec's nipples, and slips into bed next to him. Alec is indeed tired after all.

The next morning Michael awakens to find himself naked and Alec gone. He tries to remember whether they had done anything, but nothing comes to mind. As he sits up and runs his fingers through his hair, he realizes that he hasn't done any of his homework for the weekend. *Oh, shit.*

Alec appears with a breakfast tray. On it is a glass vase with a few marigolds and a porcelain teapot with a pair of matching cups quivering slightly.

"Good morning," he smiles. "You sit back." Michael looks at the tuft of chest hair poking out of his loose bathrobe.

Michael piles the pillows behind himself against the headboard and unwinds his legs to accommodate the tray on his lap. "Did we do it?"

"Did we do what?"

"I don't know how it happened. I was wearing my shirt and my briefs, and then ..." Michael holds up his hands.

"Well, I don't know how you got into my bed. Michael, you were so incredible. I've never had anyone so responsive. You were just amazing."

"I'm sorry I don't remember anything. I'd have to see you naked."

"Later. You need some tea first."

"Tea? I hate tea."

"It's not Lipton, mind you. Oh." He stops and indicates Michael's hearing aids on the tray. "Can you understand me anyway?"

"I told you, you're very easy to lipread."

"*Merci bien.*"

"What was that?" Michael puts in his hearing aids.

"Ahhh." He shakes his finger. "I spoke a little French for your benefit."

"*Merci bien?* God."

"This tea is real and authentic." He takes the cover off the teapot. "See this? There are no teabags. Real leaves, here." He pours some into their cups. "Try some. It's not too hot now."

Michael sips tentatively. The tea proves to be gentle without any acrid aftertaste.

"Like it?"

"Yes. Yes!"

"Art is not just a painting or an object. Look at the wallpaper there, and the way those dressers complement it. That's a different kind of art, and boiling tea leaves is also an art by itself." Alec sits next to him and rests an arm on his shoulders. "Making love is an art too, and you're among the best I've ever had."

"What about us?"

"Something as good as this can never last very long."

"Why not? What do you mean?"

Alec bites his lower lip. "Because. You will change. You're different; you're going to be more different. Do you understand?"

"You're saying this because you just had me?"

"No. No. You're young. You have a whole world in front of you. No. Let me change that to: You have more than one world waiting for you. As long as you're here, I'd be very happy to teach you all that I know. We can study my art books and go to museums whenever we can. I can tell that you're not getting enough appreciation at your school, so ... okay?"

"But why? Why do you want to do all this?" The tea in Michael's mouth seems abruptly bitter; he puts his cup down on the tray.

"I'm not an artist. Yes, I can talk about it. I can write about it, but I'm not the most honest critic in existence. I do not truly understand art as it is. Sometimes I make statements about art, but that's only because I want to fool myself and sound good to everybody else who doesn't take the time to know any better. I'm too afraid to live the life of an artist, someone who'll keep asking questions that take forever to answer. You're not afraid to ask. That's why you're different from me. And almost everyone else."

"What do you mean, 'almost'?"

"Because there are so few people who—you don't have any pretensions. No one's told you how art should be, and yet I think you understand it better than I do. I have far too many pretensions; I'm stuck with them because I create them for a living. But you're free to find your own voice."

"I don't understand."

"Michael. I know. Look, you can see I live very well. But that doesn't mean I am a critic of the highest order. You're the first person I've met who's cut me down to size, and you didn't even know it! I can't be with you all the time; my entire sense of worth would be wiped out. What could I possibly have left?"

"Me," Michael says.

"No, no! You don't understand! What I'm trying to say is, you will be somebody."

"Ha. I don't even have a decent portfolio."

"Well, you just have to keep working at it, that's all."

"But what about Ted?"

"Michael, I can't tell you what to do. Your passion for learning, that is the finest thing of life any artist could ever possibly ask for. Just listen to your heart and ignore those people who always have to say something negative because that's how they feel about themselves. Critics—like me—we're paid to con the public into thinking that by reading our reviews, they'll know art as well. Tell me, who's your favorite art critic?"

"Well ... I don't even know of anybody."

"That's the way it should be."

Alec looks at the Seth Thomas clock atop a lower dresser. "It's time for brunch. Oh, come on, honey-nose, we've got to move on and figure out what we can do in New York."

As Michael walks beside Alec toward Dupont Circle and ponders the wild possibility of having his work shown in New York City, he sees in the distance two Deaf men he knows. They are dressed in stone-washed jeans, LA-style T-shirts, and brand-new denim jackets; their crewcuts stand on end, moist with mousse, and their moustaches are perfectly trimmed. They sign animatedly to each other, not seeing Michael walking beside Alec from across P Street. He thinks about how the nights of these Deaf men's lives will pass in bars, how they will age and adapt by changing bars, and how they will continue to follow each other. He remembers their awkward looks when they'd tried to talk with each other at Deaf parties. *Could I truly be that different?*

"You know them?" Alec glances back again.

"Yes," Michael says finally. "Once upon a time, but not anymore. I've got better things to look for."

TRUST

Up until three days ago I had thought the world of you. You were a phenomenal interpreter because you didn't just translate what the speaker said onstage into broad strokes of Sign. You were fluent enough to insert the finer nuances of his voice throughout your interpreting so I could see not only the intent of what he said, but also the emotional thrust behind his words. I loved watching you because I knew I could trust you to convey the truth of whatever you heard. With you I never felt I was missing out on anything. Many of my Deaf friends have agreed on this about you.

Sometimes you have a hard time figuring out what the speaker is saying, because, as you've complained to us Deaf people numerous times, some hearing people do not know how to enunciate clearly. They mumble, and sometimes they don't look at the audience for long. You do better when you know what they are going to say beforehand, which is why you had done so well with musicals and plays at the Raleigh Memorial Auditorium. Theatrical interpreting is your forte.

All my life hearing people have pooh-poohed me because I wore hearing aids and couldn't speak very well. I also didn't fit the stereotype of a Deaf person being a fantastic lipreader; it was as if that part of my brain didn't function well with speechreading. My speech therapist tried very hard to improve my skills, but it was clear that I needed Sign for full access. I was part of a Deaf program that pushed its students to be mainstreamed. Even though I had a classroom interpreter, my hearing classmates made fun of me behind my back.

Hearing people have made sure that I understood I wasn't pretty or desirable enough. My body is shaped like a pear, and you can blame it on my father's side of the family. All the women have tiny chests and wide butts. When my classmates wore tight designer jeans, I felt ashamed. I couldn't wear something like that and not be called names. I wore loose shirts and skirts. I looked uncool, but no one had ever told me to my face that I didn't need to change to be worthy of love.

I was so relieved when I could finally escape to college in Washington, DC. There, Gallaudet became the home I wished I had while growing up. Deaf people were everywhere, and hearing people too could sign. It was my closest thing to Heaven on earth.

I met my husband there. Josh was kind and funny, and he said he didn't mind my outsized butt. I couldn't believe it. Of course, I fell in love with him. I'd never had a man want me as I am. Other Deaf men had made it rather clear that if I could somehow lose weight, I'd become a more attractive prospect. It was so demoralizing, but I had many Deaf women friends who knew how to make me feel better about myself. There was indeed nothing wrong with me.

Josh and I moved from DC to North Carolina when he scored a teaching job at the Eastern North Carolina School for the Deaf. I found a job at the NC Council for the Deaf and Hard of Hearing in Raleigh. We bought a house at the halfway point between Wilson and Raleigh, so it's worked out quite well for us commute-wise. Then our three kids came along.

I can tell you've never had kids. Do you know how I know? Everything you wear is expensive right down to your diamond earrings and bracelets, and you have the luxury of time to apply such immaculate makeup so your face never reveals a single flaw, so much that it seems like a mask at times. Once you have a kid of your own, everything about your life will change. You will lament never having enough money for all the things your kid needs and never having enough time for yourself. Whether you like it or not, priorities do change you.

But as long as you don't have kids, you can seem forever young.

Oh, no. Eternal youth is a fallacy. I even know your true age. You know how I know? I'm the person who files your paperwork at the council.

You may be a great interpreter, but you are a liar. Will you admit to flirting with Josh behind my back? Will you confess to having had sex with him? Has he told you secrets about me? What?

Oh, right: You've been trained in the Interpreter's Code of Ethics. You've long learned not to divulge the specifics of a job or a client's name.

Am I just another client to you?

Look at me.

I say, Look at me!

Stop pretending that I'm not there.

I specifically requested that you be booked to interpret the governor of North Carolina, who's about to step onstage and talk about providing better access to services for Deaf people across the state now that my friend Emma's won her lawsuit. Two years ago, Emma filed an embarrassing and expensive lawsuit against the state hospital system which claimed to have the right to determine when ASL interpreters would be on call, so no interpreters were available on weekends. A nice budget-saving measure, right? And Deaf people never get hurt over the weekend, of course.

As you probably know, Emma was in a horrible accident one Saturday night. A hearing drunk driver didn't press his brakes fast enough and pushed her car off the freeway. In the emergency room, she insisted on having an interpreter, but no, they would have to make do with a pen and pad. Once she recovered, she filed a lawsuit. She refused to accept the huge settlement offered to her. She insisted on continuing the suit, and she won. Good for her.

But that's not why I am sitting right here in the audience, watching you.

I want to see how you will conduct yourself now that I've just told you I know about you two.

Your word "Sorry" doesn't begin to cut it.

Oh, no.

I want you to feel the scald of my laser-fire eyes burrowing deep into the smoothness of your cheekbones.

Oh, look at you! So cool and composed, and chic as ever in a flattering black blouse. I wonder if you've dyed your hair to hide its grays creeping in. I'm not sure. I'd need to look at your hair more closely.

Alas, I'm not the only Deaf person in the audience. Five of us are sitting in the front row, and I've made a point of sitting right in the middle. I want to make it difficult for you to avoid me when it's your turn to go on stage. I am a stone-cold presence simmering with lava underneath my skin: You are just another hearing person who's already profited from mastering ASL to make a living off it, and now you felt the need to play around with my Josh? What kind of a Deaf community ally are you?

What have you done to lead him astray?

Yes, he's handsome if you don't mind his dad bod. But why couldn't you chase someone your age? Aren't you a professional cougar?

Maybe you simply enjoy taking and taking without having to face the consequences. You know you're pretty. No wrinkles or liver spots.

I somehow sense you don't want kids. Well, they will be a huge problem if you go any further with Josh. They won't like you. I know my kids.

So what did you say to lead him astray?

Answer me.

He has *kids*! *Our* kids! They're not quite teenagers yet.

Are you ready to be their cold and chic stepmother who will prove impossible to please? They're both Deaf.

Are you ready to hear Josh worry about his kids all the time when he's with you?

Just what did you say to make him feel that I wouldn't possibly know?

You see, I can tell instantly if something is bothering Josh. He doesn't need to say anything. He's an easy book to read.

I should know. I'm his *wife*.

I don't think you understand what it means to love. Marriage is the toughest form of love. Are you willing to stay with someone who can bore you out of your mind now and then, and not cheat on him?

The only thing you understand about men is the need to possess something that's not meant to be yours. Like ASL, which you wear like a mask.

You see, Josh doesn't wear guilt well.

He's since confessed to everything. He was crying in my arms. Crying!

This is a man who never cries.

If I won full custody of Tom and Anya, you'd inherit a broken man. He'll be angry at you for the rest of his life. What a great way to start a new relationship, right?

You see, we Deaf women have compared notes when our Deaf

husbands fall for hearing women who happen to be fluent in Sign. Most of them come back when they realize how awful hearing people can be. Of course they've always known this, but it's odd how easily they seem to forget this fact after having been with Deaf wives for so long.

If he changes his mind about me, will you let him live with you in your loft in the oh-so-trendy Warehouse District? Will you badger him about wearing better shoes so the two of you can fit in better with the fashionistas strutting up and down the streets?

Oh! Another question: Will you always interpret for him when you two go out to an expensive restaurant on Fayetteville Street where you'll meet up with your hearing friends?

And let me tell you something else: Josh is not an adventurous eater. He's predictable, and that's another reason why I love him. A bit boring, yes, but kids need a stable father who's not ashamed of showing his love for them.

Have you noticed the kind of clothes he wears? He's a T-shirt-and-dorky-cargo-shorts kind of guy when he's not wearing a tie and slacks. He has something of a beer belly going. He sure loves the Tar Heels. He will get very upset if you make him miss out on a Tar Heels game. He buys a season pass every year. Just saying.

And here's another thing.

He's not even sure if he loves you.

Did he ever tell you that?

Would you like to know how he knew you weren't for him?

I told him that if you were a homewrecker, there was a very good chance of you doing that again to someone else, and probably for a hearing man. Easier for you so you wouldn't have to interpret or deal with our kids all the time. More convenient, right?

I simply pointed out the fact that you've never married, and that you've most likely never known what it's like to have kids.

Knowing all this about you makes me feel good.

I smile. I may not be as pretty as you, but I'm a lioness. I have no qualms over mauling you if necessary. You are just skin and bones.

You see, Josh isn't a client.

I am.

Just stand up there and do your job and leave my husband alone.

TTY

The side table light flutters awake to the sound of my phone ringing. I wonder whether it's Ruth. I have been waiting all day for her to call and wondering whether Jack would survive his triple bypass surgery. It's been a long time since I've seen him. He's the only one in the whole world who knows how much I love him, will always love him no matter what, even if he won't leave Ruth for me.

I force the phone's receiver ends into the black suction cups of my TTY as I quickly turn the small machine on. I type, HELLO GA

IS THIS LIBBY QQ GA

YES WHO IS THIS QQ GA

RUTH HERE GA

OH GOOD HOW IS JACK DOING QQ GA

HE STILL SLEEPY DR SAID IT MAY TAKE UP 60 MINS FOR HIM WAKE UP SO I THOUGHT CALL U ANYWAY GA

THANK U THE SURGERY GO OK QQ GA

WELL DR HAD STRANGE LOOK ON HIS FACE BUT SECOND INTERPRETER NOT COME YET SO I WAIT FIRST THEN ASK DR MORE DETAIL GA

AH HOPE ITS NOTHING SERIOUS HOW R U DOING QQ GA

SCARED BUT HAVE FAITH GOD WILL TAKE CARE EVERYTHING GOD BEEN GOOD ME 27 YEARS SO IF HE DIE

She doesn't type in GA so I stare at the unblinking ribbon screen, with the teal-colored letters becoming brighter by the second so that it seems to flash like a marquee in the theater of my brain. Maybe she's crying and has forgotten to type in the GA. Or maybe the second interpreter has arrived. Or maybe the doctor has interrupted her. Or maybe something's happened to Jack and it's become an emergency.

I stare, and stare, holding my breath. My body feels like a dynamite stick ready to explode the split second she types again.

But she doesn't.

I look at my watch. Has only one minute passed?

I want to type in GA for her, but she would get really mad if I did that. I did that once to her, and she never let me forget. Later, when we met again in person, she told me that Jack thinks of me as a good friend and had told her not to get upset. She forgave me.

They live about twenty minutes away from me. Jack hasn't retired from his job at the post office, but he mentioned that he might have to. It all depends on how well his heart recovers from the surgery. He's had two heart attacks already.

The first heart attack changed him overnight. He stopped smoking, which proved to be very hard for him. He needed to do *something* with his hands, so he came over to my house and wouldn't leave my bed. I couldn't believe his ardor. I told him that he should quit smoking more often. He laughed, and then coughed. His body still craved that fume of nicotine circulating inside his lungs. The coughing eventually stopped.

Then he took to walking more often and lost some weight. Ruth stayed home because of her weak knees. She had gained some weight because she had pretty much stopped exercising. Her knees caused her a lot of pain. She hobbled around with crutches. There were moments when I envied her when I watched from outside the deaf club. Jack always hurried out of their car and walked around the front to open her door and pulled out her crutches from the back seat and lent a helping hand to lift her up. He did this quickly and smoothly as if in a single motion without pause, and all with a smile. A flicker of frustration never crossed his face. Even though I didn't want to be disabled, I wanted to be her, his wife, the true light of his life. I wanted her ring on my finger. I didn't want to be a twice-divorced woman with two cats who shared the same window overlooking the street. I didn't want to be a failure in love.

The first time I saw him was twenty-two years ago at the Deaf club. I had just moved to town to begin a new job, a new life. I was relieved that I never had children after all. I'd seen how so many of my friends tried to cope with raising their kids alone after divorce. Sometimes I babysat their kids on nights when they needed to work an occasional night shift. I could tell how broke they were, so I never charged a dime for my time. Having kids for an evening was a lot of fun, but I didn't feel wired to be a mother. But that night at the Deaf club, there was a small play performed by local community actors, which was great fun despite the fact that no one onstage could act well enough to be professional.

He was one of the actors onstage. He knew he wasn't a good performer, so he hammed it up with exaggerated movements, especially with his signs. Sometimes he forgot a line or two. Everyone in the audience clearly knew him, so they laughed along with him. I laughed too, and fell in love with him, not knowing who he was. I fervently prayed that he wasn't married.

Later, when I met him, he was standing next to Ruth. She and I had met some years ago at a National Association of the Deaf convention in my old hometown, but I hadn't met her husband then. I went up to her and introduced myself. Luckily, she remembered me.

His brown eyes never left mine as she and I bantered for a bit. I prayed that she wasn't his wife.

"Sorry," she said when she suddenly glanced at Jack. "Me-forget introduce husband."

When we shook hands, I felt a scorch of fire leaping from the sweat of his palm onto mine. I knew then that not all was lost. I had done the singles bars thing before, so it wasn't as if I hadn't had affairs before.

Later that night I made a pact with myself. After two husbands, I didn't consider myself marriage material. I could have a boyfriend, but I wouldn't marry again. I didn't want a man to try controlling me again. If he were married, then he wouldn't have much of a leash with which to control me. In fact, I could control him with the mild threat of outing our affair to his wife.

Two weeks later I ran into Jack and Ruth at the mall. We exchanged phone numbers. I wanted to fall deeper into his eyes. I was shocked by how oblivious Ruth seemed to his silences as she babbled on. I wondered if he was feeling the same-old, same-old-ness of marriage.

I asked him that question with my eyes.

A flicker of sadness appeared—and evaporated just as quickly—in his eyes. How I wanted to reassure him that he was more than all right, that he was still desirable!

I met up with Jack and Ruth for a round of card games at the Deaf club. They introduced me to a number of single Deaf men, but I wasn't all that interested. I was still too new in town to jump into a relationship with a Deaf man that no one in the community seemed to like, which, in turn, would've affected my future chances of building a viable social life there. I needed to play it slow.

I began going to the Deaf club every weekend. You could say I became something of a regular.

One night, when I was alone in the hallway after having used the restroom, I saw Jack ready to enter the men's restroom. His face suddenly lit up. He glanced around and saw that we were indeed alone. He said, "You beautiful hot. Me give-you my work number. TTY." He pulled out his small pad and pencil, and scribbled just his number. "Me work early-morning mid-afternoon. Maybe lunch meet?"

I nodded quietly. My body felt as if it was blooming with tendrils opening up petals.

There in the large room where people sat around tables and played cards, Jack acted as if he wasn't looking out for me. I took his cue and did the same. I felt so alive I thought I was burning up with a fever! But I wasn't.

That Monday I called him from my office desk where I processed insurance claims all day long. MAY I SPEAK TO JACK FOWLES PLEASE GA

HOLD ON GA

OK GA

I tried to imagine what the machines sorting the mail looked like. Were they loud like the lithograph machines almost a century before when printing presses had hired many Deaf people because the machines were that loud? HI JACK HERE WHO THIS GA

LIBBY HERE HOW R U QQ GA

U ACTUALLY CALL ME WOW ME DO GOOD HOW R U GA I felt an acute desire to transform myself into a single electron and leap into the telephone wire and shimmer like wildfire across the miles right into his thick hands typing on his TTY. I wanted him to feel my body.

I AM FINE GA

GOOD WHERE U WORK WHAT TIME U FREE LUNCH GA

The next day he showed up at my home. My office was nearby, which was why I'd chosen that apartment. We didn't talk much once he walked inside, but the passion was incredible. I hadn't believed that it was possible to have great sex with a man until Jack showed up. He made me realize how clueless I had been about the essential element of chemistry. Yes, I'd understood the concept, but until him, I hadn't experienced it. We couldn't get enough of each other.

We took to meeting twice a week at my place. This went on for the next twenty years. I was perfectly content with the arrangement. In fact, I don't think we'd ever discussed its terms and conditions. What we had was more than just sex; he probably felt that talking about our relationship itself would've destroyed whatever illusions we shared each time we met in my apartment. We never talked about Ruth.

Each time we ran into each other at the Deaf club, we always played it cool. We made sure that we didn't seem all that physically familiar with each other. In time, Ruth and I became good friends, especially when I began to learn how to quilt. I had joined a Deaf women's quilting club, and Ruth happened to be there.

Then she was in a terrible accident. A drunk driver had smashed into her car. Her knees were damaged, and she couldn't walk independently again. I felt so awful for her. I understood when Jack stopped coming by my place. It was all about pain medications and physical therapy. She eventually had to leave her job and go on disability. The pain had proven to be too much.

I felt a heave of sadness every time I saw Jack at the Deaf club. I did not know that it was possible to miss a man so much. The conversation was almost always the same.

"How Ruth doing?"

"Same-same. Some days up-down. That."

I tried to look deeply into his eyes, which he loved when we were alone together, but he averted his gaze. He glanced around. "Us-two finish ok?"

I nodded. My poker face was perfect.

I didn't know how much it would hurt to grieve the loss of an affair, but that weekend I drank and drank and drank in the angry silences of my apartment. I wanted to get drunk and die. I wanted to drive to their house and tell Ruth the truth about us. I wanted to jump off the Smith Bridge just outside of town. But there was no way to forget his presence. He breathed inside my bones. If I sighed, he sighed too. We had been that much in synchronicity.

Once, after a bout of spectacular lovemaking, he said, "If me single, me marry you would."

But he was a stickler for honoring contracts. He wasn't going to break his contract of matrimony for anyone. He'd chosen to marry Ruth, and that was that. While he understood why some people divorced, he couldn't imagine it for himself.

Now and then I began having dreams in which Ruth had somehow unexpectedly died. I would be there to comfort him through his grief. I would help him with the paperwork. We wouldn't have sex either. No one would be too surprised if we did marry a year later; it would've seemed like an inevitability.

Then he had his second heart attack right there at the Deaf club. I didn't catch him collapsing at the side of the large room facing us card players, but it seemed as if a flash of ambulance workers had suddenly appeared in the melee revolving around him. I saw him outfitted with an oxygen mask. As he was carried away quickly on a stretcher, thoughts of him being forever gone smacked me in the head. During our affair, I had hoped that we'd both outlive Ruth long enough to reconnect fully in the way it was meant to be. I knew I was growing older, as was everyone else I knew, but it was in that moment I acutely felt like I had really begun to age. I couldn't take the invincibility of my body for granted anymore.

I saw him a few weeks later. It was clear that whatever fire he had inside before had gone out. Mortality had slapped him hard in the face, and he was still stung. Nevertheless, I gave him a special smile to let him know that no matter how he might be feeling, he was still all right by me. He sighed and slowly shook his head no. Whatever we had was really over for him.

I pretended not to register what he'd said. "Everything OK? Your heart OK?"

He launched into describing what it was like to ride inside the ambulance and feel it rushing through the streets toward the hospital. He was pleasantly surprised to find that they'd arranged an interpreter not long after his arrival. He stayed the night and was sent home the next day.

That was the night I learned how to cry like never before in my life. I didn't know that love could produce so much brine full of scald.

It hurt so much that I finally said yes to a first date with Gus Burton. He had flirted with me for years, and he didn't seem to understand why I wasn't interested in him. He was a lug with a huge belly. He loved his beers too much.

A flicker of teal on the TTY's ribbon screen grabbed my attention. "Pah," I thought.

SORRY DR AND INTERPRETER WERE HERE SURGERY WENT WELL HES STILL SLEEPING BUT SHOULD WAKE UP SOON WILL LET U KNOW LATER OK QQ GA

YES THANK U CALL ME ANYTIME GA

WILL DO TALK LATER GA SK

OK SKSK

I know I've said I wasn't marriage material, but I ended up marrying Gus anyway.

Mortality can do that to you sometimes.

JOANNA'S DIARY: JUNE 12, 1999

Every summer Val always gets in the way of my friends. Nobody likes the sound of her speech. They always roll their eyes behind her back. They know I know. They understand that she's a duty I can't always get out of. I'm so happy they're my friends. I'm the only one around here who can understand her speech. It's not always easy to follow. So much depends on what we're doing at the moment. Neighbors say that I'm such a saint for putting up with her. I don't know. She's my younger sister, so I suppose I'm kind of used to her. She goes downstate to a deaf residential school in the fall and spring because no one up here knows what else to do with her. Our school here is too small for a deaf student who can't lipread well. Yeah, she has to use sign language, but I don't really know an awful lot. Just enough to get by. I mean, we get along okay. Sometimes I wish she would just go off and find friends of her own when she comes up here, but there isn't anyone who can sign in these parts. She doesn't know anything about the latest singers and movies that me and my friends love so it's a drag having to explain stuff to her all the time. She gets mad sometimes if I don't explain everything to her. Our parents don't know what to do with her either. They sit there at the table and pretend to understand everything she says. It's almost as if she's an animal to them, but she isn't, really. If she doesn't use her voice, she would look like anybody else. I mean, she doesn't contort her face strangely when she signs, but when she speaks, well, it's obvious she's making a lot of effort to talk. Sometimes it's painful to watch. She sometimes gets angry when one of my friends tries not to give her a look of disgust. Here's the thing. Her voice isn't all that pleasant. That's the honest truth. It really grates on your ears. It's got this really weird high pitch. She can't hear herself, but somehow a speech therapist had lied to her a few years ago that her speech was really excellent. She's got it into her head that she can be friends with hearing people just fine. Like me. I keep trying to explain to her that she can sound unpleasant at times, but she keeps saying, "But you're not a speech therapist. What do you know?" I hate it when she says that because it's not true. Actually, I do know a lot. I know what hearing people like when they talk with each other. They know what they want to hear when they hear a voice. I love her, but after three days of her dogging me around, I'm already wanting her to go back downstate to Flint. I know that probably makes me an awful sister, but I can't help it. I just want an easy family life like we have when she isn't home. Nobody should have to work this hard to communicate. I know she's got good friends at school, but they live all over the state. I can't wait for her to graduate from high school and marry some deaf guy so she can leave me alone.

ONE OF THE GOOD GUYS

Do I know everyone here in this bar? Oh, yeah. Which guy do you wanna meet?

Him?

Wait, wait—which one are we talking about?

The taller one with dark hair and scruffy beard and white shirt?

Okay. Everyone always asks about him when they come in here for the first time.

His name? Oh. Everyone knows him as the Deaf Guy. I know his real name, but he doesn't want anyone to know it. He prefers it that way. Damn. Look at his muscles. It's amazing how he's still got a great tone.

Me? Oh, gosh. It's been a while since I've worked out. I'm too old for that sort of thing. Arthritis, you know? See my fingers here? Too hard to lift weights now.

I've hung out in the bars long enough to notice how deaf guys get around. When I came out, they used a notepad and pen. Nowadays, if a hearing guy wants to chat with a deaf guy, they exchange their numbers and text each other even though they're standing right next to each other. It's kind of cute sometimes, when one of them looks up and smiles at the other, and then goes back to texting.

But all of the deaf guys leave town once they graduate from high school. There's nothing for deaf people here. We don't even have an ASL interpreter around here. The town's too small for even this gay bar, but we got guys who need family here.

Oh yeah. Sometimes the Deaf Guy and I will text each other a bit when we're both bored. I'm just a backup buddy. Most of the time we just wave hello to each other and that's it for the rest of the night. I have my own buddies, and he has his own text buddies.

Oh, sure. You can go ahead and talk with him. I don't think he will mind talking with you. He tends to prefer guys who work out, though. Just wanted to point that out.

I do feel bad for him sometimes. I think he's the only deaf gay guy in town. Well, maybe not, but I haven't seen other deaf guys show up here. No one signs.

I asked him once, Why don't you move out to Minneapolis? A bigger city, you know?

He said, Can't. Turned out that he had to take care of his mother. Maybe cancer? Not sure. But she's disabled. Can't move around much, even with a wheelchair. They live six blocks over from Clark School. He gets an occasional night off, so he comes here. A little diversion, you know?

Well, yeah. But he's a really good guy. Here's why I know. I've met his mother. She doesn't really sign. She's also not a nice person, but he knows that he's got to take care of her like any good son would. That's the kind of guy a man should want, but don't because ... well, he's deaf! That pisses me off sometimes, the way some hearing guys treat him like nothing.

I should know. Yeah, we had a small thing going at one time back when I was still working out. I tried so hard to learn how to sign, but you know, the real problem was me. I kept expecting him to lipread everything. I didn't understand how hard it could be to lipread. I was just an arrogant prick. I was really hot stuff back then. Took me a long time to lick my own wounds. I didn't want to admit that I was totally wrong. I had too much pride.

Yeah, I did apologize to him, but the damage was done. He was tired of having hearing guys trying to control the relationship.

So yeah, I was one of those assholes.

Yeah. Do I look like an asshole? Me, an asshole. Who'd have believed it? But yeah, I screwed it up.

Do I still sign? I wish. I just know the alphabet and that's it. I did know a few signs, but you know how it is. If you don't use it, you lose it, you know? I do remember this one, though: *You handsome*. It's all about the face. Nice, eh?

Oh, he'd be happier with a boyfriend who actually signs. Not just someone who goes, *Hey I know sign language!* And all they know is the alphabet. Sign language is a lot more than the alphabet.

Well, yes, guys say they want to learn sign language, but it's not the same thing. Do you really want to teach your hearing boyfriend sign language? What about real communication, the heavy lifting stuff that's required to make a relationship work? He wants a boyfriend boyfriend, not an ASL student boyfriend.

You can't just want him. You have to be willing to take ASL classes, and the nearest one is about forty-five minutes from here. Are you willing to make that kind of commitment?

So if he likes you, consider yourself damn lucky. I'll try my best not to get jealous. He's one of the really good guys here.

Just don't you dare break his heart. If you do, I'm coming after you. I'm not joking. Everyone here knows that I won't put up with anyone hurting him. *Ever*. Do you understand?

Good!

Good luck.

THE MOMENT WHEN I DIED

The moment when I died was the first time I understood everything I'd misunderstood for so long I wanted to head back and apologize and make amends.

My entire life became a reel that spun a million revolutions per second, and yet everything was crystal clear, as if in slow motion.

It was surreal to see myself as a little girl, and to see my body metamorphosing into that of a young woman. Did I really look like her?

I had been so long accustomed to seeing myself as an old woman that the shock of seeing so much youth in her face, in her movements, lingered for a long time afterward, filtering through the spectacle of middle age when my son Derek sneered at me. "You're not a good mother, Mom. You never were."

Oh, how those words hurt.

The way his nasal speech, emptied of most consonants, had echoed over and over again in my dreams. How could he make such a vile accusation? Hadn't I toiled so hard to make sure that all our kids were fed? What a selfish thing to say after all I'd done for him!

No matter how much I'd prayed to God for intervention, my son refused to return for even a short visit.

Five years later, I died.

The moment when I died was the first time I realized how different my new world would become after traveling three hours to have Derek's hearing tested in an audiology clinic at the university. Jim and I had suspicions that Derek had a hearing problem, but we weren't sure. He didn't seem to know his name when we called him to dinner. His doctor suggested that we get his hearing tested.

Our appointment was with Mr. Wevill, an older audiologist who was due to retire at any moment. Something about his casual suit and loosened tie made me feel that I could trust him.

In the big glassed-in room, Derek fidgeted on a small chair. A small number of plush toys covered with loud colors distracted him. It was tough to test his hearing. He didn't seem to understand that he was supposed to raise his hand each time he heard a sound in his headphones. He also tried to push the headphones off his head. A young woman, who was a graduate student in the audiology department, sat patiently with him, trying to redirect his attention to the sounds that were beeping into his ears.

Watching Derek and the young woman while sitting next to Mr. Wevill as he rotated his dials and notated the X's and O's across Derek's first audiogram chart, I felt like a mass of nerves with nowhere to go but everywhere to scream. How I wanted him to raise his hand!

But I kept my face calm as porcelain. I would not show anyone the storm of emotions ranging inside me. After all, I was his mother, and he needed to know who was in charge.

I was so relieved when the woman finally brought Derek back into Mr. Wevill's office. He ran right into my arms. I almost cried.

Then came the diagnosis. After looking quickly at the audiogram, Mr. Wevill said, "Well, looks like he's profoundly deaf. Derek's gonna need hearing aids."

I inhaled. I would not cry.

Derek wasn't even two years old. He seemed to have forgotten already having worn headphones. I immediately held him close to my chest. "How's he going to survive?" I didn't know that I would hug him differently than any of my five other kids.

I fell into a blur of worrying about Derek's future and taking him back to Mr. Wevill, another three-hour trip each way, when his first pair of earmolds came in, and I watched him trying to pull them out.

Mr. Wevill sighed and used a nail file to narrow down the earmold's thickness so it could fit better inside his ear.

Then Derek pulled out both of his earmolds and unbuckled his hearing aid, which was bulky and rechargeable. He threw everything onto the floor.

My heart stopped. "Derek!"

The audiologist chuckled. "He doesn't understand why he's supposed to wear them. Hold on a sec." He pulled out a binder from a shelf near his desk. There were pictures of young kids wearing hearing aids. He brought it down to Derek and pointed to the pictures. "These. Are deaf kids. You. Look. This is you!"

Derek stared at the pictures for a full minute. He had never stopped to stare at anything for long. He was always glancing around, looking.

"But …"

"Shhh," Mr. Wevill said. "He has to feel that it's all up to him."

Derek glanced back at the floor where his hearing aid was. He picked it up and looked at it. He turned it around and around. It was clear that it didn't look like the same hearing aids that the deaf children wore in the pictures.

Mr. Wevill bent down to the floor and pulled up the earmolds by their cords. He directed Derek's eyes back to the picture and pointed to the deaf children's ears. Every one of them was wearing earmolds with cords attached to their hearing aids solidly in front of their small chests.

A few minutes later Mr. Wevill was able to put the earmolds back into Derek's ears and adjusted the straps containing his first hearing aid. He looked directly into Derek's eyes and pointed to his hearing aid.

When Derek looked down at his hearing aid, Mr. Wevill tapped the top of it gently.

Derek looked at me, startled. It was the first sound he heard clearly using a hearing aid.

I was never prouder of him than in that moment.

The moment when I died was the first time I sat down with Mrs. Niller, Derek's new speech therapist. She was among the many young and eager women I'd meet over the years when it came to his education, and I liked her right off the bat. Nothing seemed to faze her, and she laughed easily.

I brought Derek to an empty classroom at an elementary school not far from where we lived. Classes had been dismissed for the day, but Mrs. Niller was willing to start Derek early on his speech therapy. He was still too young to go to school.

By then Derek had seemed to accept his hearing aid. His brothers and sisters found his hearing aid to be weird, but in time they stopped saying anything about it. Derek strapped it onto his chest like most people with bad vision would put on their glasses at the start of the day. I couldn't always tell if he heard anything, but there were times when I saw a flicker of puzzlement when he heard something new and different, like a sharp caw from across the street.

I tried to tell him. "You just heard a crow. Over there." I rushed him to the front window where our street was lined with tall trees where crows liked to perch. He still looked confused when I pointed up to the trees and tried to explain. It was clear on his face that he understood he was quite different from us.

At the school, Mrs. Niller opened a full-color book that had words set in bold type beneath each illustration.

Derek sat next to me as she pointed to each picture. "Man," she said.

"Woman."

"Boy."

"Girl."

"Dog."

"Cat."

But he didn't seem to understand what he was supposed to do.

"Come over here," she said.

Derek walked around the table to her.

"Now," she said. "Just feel this." She took his hand and brought it up to her throat. "Bum-bum-bum!"

He stopped, then looked at me.

I pointed to my own throat and said, "Bum-bum-bum!"

She repeated, "Bum-bum-bum!"

He opened his mouth and tried to make movements.

She whipped out a small mirror and held it up to their faces close together. "Look. Bum-bum-bum!"

She brought his hand to her throat, then to his own.

His first utterance sounded so timid. "Bub-bub-bub."

"Yes! You got it!"

She and I looked at each other with glee.

"Bub-bub-bub! Bub-bub-bub!"

He was such a good student that I didn't fear that he'd try to learn sign language.

*

The moment when I died was the first time I was forced to wonder whether it was fair to any of my kids to be part of a large family.

My husband Jim was often too tired to do anything when he got home from the warehouse. He worked six days a week, not five, because he needed the extra money to help pay for the house and the kids. He had wanted to have a large family, but I don't think he'd understood just how expensive that was going to be.

I didn't understand at the time how large families can exact a terrible price that has nothing to do with money. No child gets enough individual attention. Someone always gets left behind.

The moment when I died was the first time I realized that the town where I grew up wasn't big enough to provide the education Derek needed. I didn't want him to move away for months at a time where he'd live downstate at a Deaf residential school. I didn't want him to turn into a stranger.

Mrs. Niller said that he was learning new words all the time, and more than that, he was *retaining* them. He remembered how to pronounce the new words correctly. He was even learning how to read sentences.

He gradually learned how to speak English. He still mispronounced some words. Most of his consonants were missing, but he was still understandable.

Each time he spoke clearly and naturally, it felt like a cause for celebration.

I now understand that during those days, my son began to wonder about me. Why wasn't I paying attention to him like before?

I was so busy with cooking and feeding and washing clothes and taking the kids to the doctor and dentist that I eventually stopped paying as much attention to Derek as I had before.

He still spoke as before, but it'd never occurred to me that he wasn't part of the happy babble around the table at mealtimes. No one paid attention to him.

When I allow myself to *really* look at his face at those times in the reel of my life, I feel a stab in my heart. It really hurts.

The moment when I died was the first time Jim and I brought Derek to his foster family who lived two hours away from home but close to a speech program for deaf kids. The new town was almost the same as mine, but it was more centrally located for other deaf kids in the region. They, too, would stay with foster families.

The Sundays seemed like a nice family. Mr. Sunday was the vice principal at the local high school, and Mrs. Sunday was a part-time teacher's aide who worked with disabled kids at Derek's new elementary school. Their three kids had all grown up and gone away. Mrs. Sunday said that she would pick him up every day after school, and she was glad to take care of him. She wasn't a grandmother yet, but she was eager to get started on her grandmothering.

Leaving him with the Sundays was the hardest decision of my life. I felt ripped in half. I didn't know if I could trust such strangers like that. I didn't understand that he would inevitably compare his foster family with our family and wonder why they couldn't be the same. Jim held my hand while I cried on our way back home.

Because Derek was the only child in their house, he got the attention he craved. There were only the three of them at mealtime. Sometimes their adult kids would visit from out of town, but Mrs. Sunday was quite emphatic about them looking directly at Derek each time they spoke.

In those days, long-distance calls were very expensive. Mrs. Sunday wrote newsy letters to me every week, which she gave to Derek to give to me.

I didn't understand how it was possible for her to say that he was such a bright and happy boy because when he came home with a college student every weekend, he seemed a bit listless. Was he really happy up there? Or was Mrs. Sunday lying to me in order to make me feel better about leaving Derek alone with them?

The moment when I died was the first time I felt quiet jolts of pride when Janey Mitchell, who lived down the street from us, remarked, "Your son's doing real well. I can tell. He speaks so good!"

That gave me hope.

I couldn't wait for him to come home every Friday, and I didn't want him to leave every Sunday afternoon.

His weekly absences left a hole that I pretended didn't exist. Having to take care of a house filled with my other five kids and a husband helped some, but not much.

*

The moment when I died was the first time I finally understood why Derek had become so angry.

The more he learned to speak, the more he asked me what was going on at the dinner table. The banter was rapid-fire. I couldn't keep up, but I couldn't stop laughing. My kids were so funny!

I didn't know that the most toxic four words for a deaf kid in a hearing household with no signing were "I'll tell you later."

Even more damning were the equally toxic four words "I'm sorry I forgot."

Those years when all of the kids lived at home went by like a blur, and I hadn't realized how often I said those words. Over and over again.

And yet we expected him to sit there and pretend he was able to follow the jokes leapfrogging all over the table.

Over and over *again.*

And yet we wanted to believe that he was such an expert lipreader that he didn't need any help at mealtime. The fact that none of us had ever wondered why he never laughed with us horrifies me now. I have no physical body of my own now, but if I did, it would've been filled with the hot fire of shame.

The moment when I died was the first time when Derek, now a full-grown man, came home for Christmas after his first semester away at college. I didn't want him to attend Gallaudet because it was full of Deaf people who signed, but it was the only college he wanted to attend. He was among the very few students who had scored a full four-year scholarship. I was so proud of him that I wanted to frame that letter congratulating him on the scholarship.

Seeing him leave our house again for college tore me up all over again. I didn't want him to leave. And Washington, DC, was a big city! How was he going to cope?

That December when he returned, the changes in him were startling and frightening. He was no longer quiet. He sported a full beard. He wore a T-shirt and an old tweed jacket he found in a thrift shop. He was upfront about using sign language even when he used his voice. He made sure that his presence was felt. He demanded to know what *all* of us were saying. None of us knew what to do, what to make of him.

I didn't understand that we'd expected him to stay quiet in the background, the way he always was at the dinner table. I didn't understand that the point of college was not to earn a degree. College was supposed to encourage independent thinking.

I hadn't grasped how independently Derek had been thinking all those years when he lived at home. Growing up, he just didn't know the words to describe those thoughts then. Being among other Deaf people his age gave him the confidence that I hadn't realized I didn't want him to have after all. He wasn't alone with his feelings.

I didn't like thinking about sign language. It was too distracting. It meant that the user was a speech failure.

My son had excellent speech! Why was he so adamant about using ASL? Why did he feel like he had to make a political statement with everything he said? Couldn't he be quiet and normal like before?

Why was he throwing away all those years he'd spent learning how to speak clearly?

I didn't appreciate his ingratitude.

The moment when I died was the first time I turned down the one chance I had to reconnect with Derek. The local community college had been offering ASL classes, and since I was officially a senior citizen, I was eligible to take the class for free.

Derek insisted that I go. "It's free!"

I shook my head no. "My hands are too stiff now. My fingers. See?" I showed him how I was developing arthritis in my hands. Which wasn't exactly true. It just looked too complicated for me. I didn't want to feel stupid.

He said, "You can adapt. I even know a Deaf guy who has only one hand. It's not a problem for him. We understand him just fine."

"Nah," I said. "Too much work."

I didn't catch how he nearly bit his own lip.

I wouldn't realize until after I'd died that that was the moment he began to question seriously why he had bothered to come home and visit with me and Jim in the first place. He had spent many years learning how to speak with us, but I couldn't be bothered to learn how to sign a few things?

It would be a few years before I saw him again.

The moment when I died was the last time I saw him leave my house. Jim had died the year before, so Derek had come to spend a weekend with me. He had been recently promoted to a new job that involved data analysis at some corporation. I never understood exactly what he did for a living, but it paid well.

In the beginning, we talked easily. He wanted to know what was up with each of his siblings and their kids.

At the kitchen table we talked and talked about relatives who'd died a long time before.

I told him stories that I hadn't realized he never heard before because he couldn't follow the family babble at the dinner table years ago.

Then we fell into a horrible argument. I had said that I was surprised he didn't know the story about Uncle Harry and his first wife's death.

He said, "How would I know? Everybody was yakking at the same time!" He paused. "Hearing people are selfish, period."

That set me off. I explained that we hearing people didn't have to help deaf people like him learn how to speak, but we did anyway. That I didn't understand what he'd truly meant would become the biggest regret of my life.

"Really? I can't believe you said that. As if you're doing me a *fucking* favor!"

The crude language shocked me. "Don't you dare use—"

"You're not a good mother, Mom. You never were."

"What?"

"You could've told everyone to stop talking all at once! Set up rules for talking at the table."

"I can't—"

"No. You could've, but you didn't want to. You didn't feel you could tell us kids how to behave, but you. *Could*. Have! But you didn't. I don't feel close to my brothers and sisters because they don't take the time to talk to me! I'm too much work."

"Derek—"

"You know how things could've been better? Because when

I stayed with the Sundays, they always made sure I understood everything at the table! It's not hard."

"But when you've got five kids—"

"You and Dad were the *adults*. You didn't tell them to stop and listen! I'm so, *so* tired of hearing people making excuses when they should know better. Nobody *listens* in this family! I'm done." He left the kitchen.

"Wait—"

But it was too late. I heard him storm upstairs to his old room where he stayed for a while.

I figured that he had needed to calm down for a bit.

I didn't know it then, but he was packing his suitcase and texting for a cab ride to a motel.

I sat in the living room, trying to watch some TV.

Then I heard his footsteps go down the stairs and leave through the kitchen and the side door outside.

Then I heard a car park in front of my house.

I hurried to the front window and peered through the curtain.

He didn't look back at the house as he got into the cab.

It was the last time I would see him while I was still alive.

The moment when I died was the first time I felt so painfully helpless without Jim. He had always comforted me when I went on and on about Derek. "He'll come around," he said. "Just give him time."

Then I told my kids about the awful things Derek had said.

They said, "You're a great mother. You really took care of us!"

They agreed that Derek had anger management issues. "Why does being deaf have to be such a big deal? He should just get over it and grow up."

I wasn't quite so sure, but I didn't want to think about it. It was much easier to go to Mass every morning and pray to God for Derek to seek forgiveness. He'd see that I wasn't a bad mother at all.

The moment when I died was the first time I blinked to see Derek one last time.

Sitting with a few other people around a long table in an Indian restaurant, Derek was holding a bald man's hand and laughing with him. I was stunned to see that he was with a *man*. Everyone at their table was quiet while a hearing woman shared a funny story about her father and his dog. She spoke and signed.

It was clear that some of the people at the table didn't sign, and some didn't speak. I was astonished by how civilized their conversation was. There were no interruptions. Ever.

Everyone listened.

That was a revelation.

Watching them, I envisioned a new kind of peace that I never knew could exist. The kind of peace that Jim and I never gave him. The kind of law and order we could've maintained at mealtimes, demanding that each person be heard with no interruptions.

I was surprised to learn that Derek was gay, but not quite so. He'd never spoken a word about who he was dating. I never asked.

Because I *knew*. Every mother knows.

But I didn't want to know.

Yet there it was: Derek was smiling radiantly. I had never seen such light emanating from any of my kids. His aura, lilting in soft rainbow hues, was quite warm and magnificent and powerful.

So much light! Who knew?

How could anyone have overlooked that about him?

And his boyfriend had a similar aura. Their auras throbbed together.

And I'd thought Derek dabbled in only resentment and darkness.

Watching my son, I knew what was coming next. His sister Carla had been trying to text him with the news that I'd died.

I'd been with her when I died in that awful hospital room. I hated the sound of my own heaves while trying to breathe.

In that disconnect between soul and body, the weight of cancer in my body was suddenly air.

I was flabbergasted by how freely I could move. I could slip through anything. Anyone alive I wanted to see, I was there in a blink.

That was how I blinked and found Derek. He looked older and a bit heavier than I recalled. It was still a shock to think of him as middle-aged, but he was. I had no idea what he'd done in the last five years before I died. I only hoped that he had been happy the whole time.

I blinked back to Carla, still trying to text. She was swearing to herself for not being able to reach Derek. I suddenly realized that he had to have blocked all of us from texting him.

Then I remembered that my youngest daughter Nancy would have his voice relay number.

I blinked back to Nancy. She had been sobbing. I whispered into her ear. "Try his voice relay number."

I blinked back to Carla just as her phone rang. It was Nancy. "Have you gotten ahold of Derek yet?"

"No! I think he's blocked me, too," Carla said.

"Okay. Let me try his voice relay number. Be right back."

I blinked back to Derek at the restaurant.

The man had just kissed Derek lovingly on the lips. He had a nice smile. I got the sense that these two were engaged to be married. I looked closely at the man. Was he good enough for my son? He looked to be about the same age as Derek.

Then Derek signed, *Marry where?*

I was startled by the fact that I could understand his signing perfectly. How was that possible? Did it mean that I had become all-knowing, like God?

Then Derek pulled his phone from his shirt pocket and set it against his wineglass. *Hi who call?*

I rushed to look at his screen. A woman in a black blouse was translating Nancy's voice into ASL. "Hi, Derek. This is Nancy. I just want you to know that Mom died a few minutes ago."

W-h-a-t? the interpreter voiced him.

"She had cancer in the bowels."

He paused. *W-o-w.*

"Yeah. Look, we're talking about having a funeral for her on Friday, so if you could come up by then, that'd be awesome. It'd be so good to see you."

Oh. Let-me think-about-it. Call-you b-a-c-k later will.

"Okay. We're still family. Remember that. Mom always wanted you to know that."

Rage flickered across his face as he slid the screen shut. *Family?* he signed to himself. *Hypocrites! W-t-f.*

His aura suddenly dampened into the graying and reddening colors of grief and anger. He looked ready to glow outward in the crimson of blood.

Who that? his boyfriend signed.

Derek signed and spoke at the same time. "My mother just passed away. Bowel cancer."

His friends signed awkwardly, *Wow so-sorry!*

His boyfriend slid around the table to sit next to him on the bench. He pulled Derek into his arms as my son sobbed.

Of course, I didn't want Derek to suffer, but it was satisfying to see that I was still a part of him, that he did have some feelings for me. I had long wondered if he still loved me.

It was all the proof I had needed.

The moment I died was the first time I began to grasp the full damage of what I'd done. Having no one alive on Earth to hear my lamentations was a new kind of hell.

I was that awful hearing mother who had thought learning ASL would be a waste of time.

I never asked him what *he* needed to be happy. How could I have been so selfish?

He didn't show up at my funeral. That really stung.

He's even changed his last name to his husband's.

He has thoroughly scrubbed his memory of me from his bones.

I am nothing. Not even a small puff of wind.

I have no voice left at the bountiful table of his life.

YEARS PASSING BY

Falling in clandestine love thirty-six years before, Betty and Gina pretty much stopped making love when their three adopted children came along in rapid order. The women taught them the language of hands and tossed them into the web of their Deaf friends who understood their relationship and their children, who were often hearing but knew the language too, on weekends and at the Deaf club downtown. All this left the pair feeling too exhausted for sex. No wonder, then, Betty and Gina never suspected the other's desire to be desired was intact; still thriving and throbbing after those early years with babies, even.

When more and more of their Deaf gay friends came out of the closet, they did, too, nervously at first, but proudly and loudly at last.

In time Betty had an affair with a Deaf school bus driver; Gina, her best friend's girlfriend. The other never knew. Both affairs did not last. The fear of a tarnished reputation was much too strong. They spent holidays with their children, hardly remembering that sharp thrill of someone other than the one at home, of breaking the sameness of their lives with urgent tongues, but when it did happen, they recomposed themselves on their way home in their cars afterwards, grateful that they were considered attractive at all, sexy enough to be lusted after. But in those short-fused affairs, they never once grumbled about the other, or even of love; just a need being fulfilled, nothing more than scratching an itch to make it go away.

In time, the children of theirs and their Deaf friends grew up, moved out, and sometimes returned only once a year or two. Now that their youngest child has graduated from college and found a job in a city much bigger than theirs, Betty and Gina's house is strangely empty.

Alone, at last, in bed, Betty and Gina feel awkward, not knowing quite what else to say. Of course, during the day, they talk a great deal about everything; it's almost as if each is a videotape camera, constantly recording without judgment, for the crime of lust if revealed would be unforgivable. They know exactly how the other would sign; in fact, their divergent styles have converged into a hybrid mode of signing.

Betty is about to turn off the bedside lamp when Gina suddenly places her hand on her arm.

"What?"

"Me-sorry." Gina's eyes brim with tears.

"Why?"

"We-two s-o old. Our youth finish."

They kiss, shocked wordlessly by the ways the other's body has aged, going flaccid, since their last intimate touch. It has been so long since they touched each other down there; the easy tautness of youth is nowhere to be felt. Their hands, now acquiring the first solidifying wrinkles and tan liver spots, rotate all over each other's bodies until the years of waiting to be loved again turn into quiet intense fireworks, never fading from the darkening skies.

ACROSS THE STREET FROM YOU

We Deaf people live across the street from you two. We do not know your first names, but we have figured out the most important thing already: You are hearing. The way you two talk to each other without looking into each other's faces is a dead giveaway. Hearing people are always afraid of being open with their words, their eyes, their faces. We notice such details because with each potential friend or neighbor, we search for any tell-tale sign, such as hearing aids discreetly hidden under the hair, or hands unconsciously fingerspelling out loud, or eyes constantly monitoring the action around them. You two are married, in your late thirties, tan and beautiful with bright white teeth and well-manicured nails; you look like you'd make fascinating friends, for you'd be the type to have traveled to Europe several times.

From watching you discreetly through our front curtains, we decide that you, Mr. Smithgow, must be a doctor, or a medical specialist of some kind; the way your hair is trimmed every week is our best clue to who you are. You do not wear a suit or tie, but you do dress well, with clothes purchased from Eddie Bauer and ordered from L.L. Bean; you probably wear this under a white lab coat at a hospital nearby. We have seen the delivery men press your buzzer and then leave permission slips with you. They return the next day, pick up your signatures, and leave your packages, often right out in the open, next to your side door. The fact that no one steals them makes us feel good about our choice to leave a large city for a smaller town like ours. And you, Mrs. Smithgow, must be a professor of archaeology or sociology at the local community college, but we haven't had a chance to check the course listings to see if you teach there. You are beautiful, with a nice strong jaw that's short of masculine; you have wonderful laugh wrinkles around your eyes. We wonder if you have children, but we see no evidence of toys or young adults who resemble either one of you. No one visits you. Of course, we don't dare approach you. After all, we don't want to give the impression that we're nosy folks. We are your new neighbors.

*

The distance you maintain with each other is carefully gauged from the second you two step outside to the driveway. The distance never changes as one of you locks the house and the other unlocks your maroon Saab. In the car you two sit carefully, wearing seatbelts to prevent the two of you from ever crashing into each other. Your bodies have become no-fly zones where spontaneous affection is forbidden.

After you leave, we discuss you two, deciphering the nuances of your body language. We wonder if you two have observed us talking, laughing, hugging our Deaf friends when they park in front of our house. They inquire after you two and our other neighbors, but we really have nothing much to say. We are still settling in, what with many boxes left to unpack. We are also hectic with our new jobs, working deeper within the Deaf community here. It is so much better where we are now, for we no longer have to strain our voices with hearing bosses and coworkers, and we find it hard to believe that we now own our first house. In the city where we once lived, we paid exorbitant rents. No more, we agreed, when both of our job offers from this new town came a day apart. Fate, we decided; and left.

At five o'clock, we come home from our jobs on the opposite ends of the town, so it becomes something of a game when we hurry just to see who gets to park first in the driveway, and who parks on the street in front of our house. Sometimes when we arrive home at the same time, we kiss each other in front of our house. Then we find you two standing on either side of your Saab, scarcely looking at each other and walking past it to the front door.

It used to be that hearing people would fret about the quality of Deaf people's lives, demanding that we learn how to speak and use our ears to partake in the joy of their culture, but now more and more of them are learning to leave us alone, only because we are indeed happy to be as we are. Perhaps they stopped bothering us so much because they saw how well we could communicate, even bluntly, and how little direct honesty they have in their own lives. We wonder out loud about the lives you two must lead in that house.

Our first winter here comes. Everyone had warned us about the amount of snow, but we are happy, cozier still when we see the text announcement of yet another day of closings for schools and stores on television. We like staying inside with our fireplace burning so hypnotically, feeling our toes heating up inside the cocoons of our slippers. We can't stop watching the purity of snow heaving softly like goose feathers below. Back in the city, the snow always turned gray within an hour of landing. But up north, the whiteness dazzles our eyes nonstop, and both of our boys and their fiancées spend Christmas with us. They, too, remark endlessly on the extreme cold, but they also comment on the perfect combination of snow and Christmas. Our two boys, now in college, agree that everything has turned out amazingly well for us.

After we attend the holiday services at our Deaf church, we come home, put wood in the fireplace, exchange presents, and show videos taken when the boys were young; we all comment on how their fluency in signs has changed since then. Their hearing girlfriends nod nonchalantly, still overwhelmed by the signing in our Deaf church. It's clear that these women will never understand the very quality that has defined our lives. Our boys' eyes mist, knowing this, and we hug them without saying a word. When it is their time to leave, we stand out on the driveway. We hug our boys tightly, this time with tears. We wish they'd marry Deaf women, but we know we can't control their hearts.

We look up and see the two of you bundled up in ski jackets and fashionable boots, waiting to unlock your chilled Saab. Just before you two step inside and buckle up, you nod acknowledgement of our presence and wave.

We wave back with smiles. We do not go into our house until your car disappears down the snow-banked street.

The snow melts, and the full fragrance of spring makes our dog jaunty. We went to the shelter when, over our Valentine's Day dinner at a fancy steak joint, we realized how much we kept talking about dogs. That night we vacuumed and corralled our extension cords. The next day, after work, we were ready to adopt. The dog who demanded to be ours, with his alert eyes watching our signing, wagged his feathery tail and sat at attention in his cage. Then he flounced around, as if he wanted to show off his gorgeous spotted coat. He sat at attention, and we looked at each other. Within thirty minutes, we three were completely in love. We discovered quickly how much Leopold loved being brushed in front of the fireplace; we didn't know how much until we felt his throat humming.

We stroll together with Leopold past eight houses down the street to the dog park. Both the fence and the gravel are somewhat tatty, as the town hasn't had the money to improve most of the older parks, but then again, it's not quite time for annual outdoor repairs.

Once inside the dog run, we unleash Leopold. He sniffs and races after the other dogs. As we sit down on a bench, his new friends sniff us over. In the distance, we catch sight of you, Mrs. Smithgow, walking alone, clearly lost in your thoughts. You are wearing a bright blue windbreaker and a pair of boots, as some park trails are still muddy. We trade glances with each other. We want so much to ask you if you are indeed all right, but you don't notice us. You go right by, disappearing through a matted cluster of trees that have begun their first shoots. We wonder why until we remember the park's restrooms are over there.

Some other dog owners come over to us and, in asking us which dog belongs to us, discover that we are Deaf. Of course, they feel awkward with their mouths and hands. We are used to this, so we point to Leopold. We clap twice, and Leopold stops, cocks his ears. We clap twice again, and he springs haughtily over to us. The dog owners are impressed, even trying to copy our signs. We scratch Leopold behind the ears, give him half a dog biscuit, and then he sprints off with his pack of friends again.

You return from the restroom. On the sidewalk alongside the dog run, you see us signing.

You do not wave.

We see the subtle glint in your eyes, as if you are ready to ignore us but can't; it'd be too rude. We stop talking and turn to you, ready to invite you somehow, but you are gone. We look at each other, wishing to absolve somehow the unsaid pain in your walk.

A group of our Deaf friends from the city where we used to live crowds our house for the Memorial Day weekend. We're immensely touched by how much they've missed us. They can barely hide their envy at the spaciousness of our backyard as we barbecue ribs and serve beer.

They are surprised to see our other hearing neighbors waving and gesturing clumsily from their backyards to us their simple gladness in seeing us having a nice time. It would seem to anyone that we have earned everything at last, but not quite. We live across the street from your house, which is now empty and up for sale.

ACKNOWLEDGMENTS

The following stories have previously appeared in these journals and anthologies:

Breath & Shadow: "Raspberries."
Clerc Scar: "Poster Child" (retitled "Poster Child '95") and "Tasting Fire."
Creatures of Habitat: A Main Street Rag Anthology (Alice Osborn, ed.; Main Street Rag): "Across the Street from You."
Crossing Lines: A Main Street Rag Anthology (Rayne Debski, ed.; Main Street Rag): "Winterlove."
Deaf Lit Extravaganza (John Lee Clark, ed.; Handtype Press): "XPT556."
The Deaf Poets Society: "Neighbors."
The Deaf Way II Anthology: A Literary Collection by Deaf and Hard of Hearing Writers (Tonya M. Stremlau, ed.; Gallaudet University Press): "How to Become a Backstabber."
Eyes of Desire 2: A Deaf GLBT Reader (Raymond Luczak, ed.; Handtype Press): "Years Passing By."
Glitterwolf: "Someone Else's Father."
I'll Tell You Later: Deaf Survivors of Dinner Table Syndrome (Raymond Luczak, ed.; Handtype Press): "The Moment When I Died."
Nothing Without Us (Cait Gordon and Talia C. Johnson, eds.; Renaissance): "Mafia Butterfly."
No Walls of Stone: An Anthology of Literature by Deaf and Hard of Hearing Writers (Jill Jepson, ed.; Gallaudet University Press): "The Finer Things."
St. Sebastian Review: "Revival."
The Tactile Mind Quarterly: "The Healing Touch," "The Language of Home," "My Martyrdom" (retitled "My Martyrdom '06"), and "Sallie Ann."

*

This collection has taken me nearly 40 years to put together. I remain in eternal gratitude to those who've helped me with this book in ways large and small along my winding journey to this very page: John Lee Clark, David Cummer (*in memoriam*), Katie Lee, Richard McCann (*in memoriam*), Deirdre Mullervy, Eric Thomas Norris, André Pellerin (*in memoriam*), Anthony Santos (*in memoriam*), and Tom Steele. But more than anyone, Melainie Wilding Garcia (*in memoriam*) was the one who'd encouraged me to pursue writing short stories more seriously back in 1985.

I also thank Bex Freund, Lilah Katcher, Rachel C. Mazique, Jeremy Quiroga, and Cynthia Weitzel for their support while I worked on this book as part of the Deaf Artist Residency Program at the Anderson Center for Interdisciplinary Arts in Red Wing, Minnesota.

ABOUT THE AUTHOR

Raymond Luczak is the author and editor of over thirty-five books, including *A Quiet Foghorn: More Notes from a Deaf Gay Life*, *From Heart into Art: Interviews with Deaf and Hard of Hearing Artists and Their Allies*, and the award-winning Deaf gay novel *Men with Their Hands*. His poetry collections *once upon a twin* and *Animals Out-There W-i-l-d* were selected as Top Ten U.P. Notable Books of the Year for 2021 and 2024. The anthologies that he's edited include *I'll Tell You Later: Deaf Survivors of Dinner Table Syndrome* and *Yooper Poetry: On Experiencing Michigan's Upper Peninsula*. His work has appeared in *Poetry*, *Prairie Schooner*, and elsewhere. An inaugural Zoeglossia Poetry Fellow, he lives in Minneapolis, Minnesota.